Billy Moon

R. Allen Chappell

Dedication

Billy Moon, book thirteen of the Navajo Nation Mysteries, is dedicated to the many loyal readers who have supported this series over the years. Their emails and letters of support have been a daily source of inspiration in the writing of this book.

Acknowledgments

As always, many sincere thanks to those Navajo friends and classmates who still provide "grist for the mill." Their insight into Navajo thought and reservation life helped fuel a lifelong interest in the culture. One I had once only observed from the other side of the fence.

Author's Note

In the back pages, you will find a small glossary of Navajo words and terms used in this story, the spelling of which may vary somewhat, depending on which experts' opinion is referenced. The Navajo language has changed over the years, as have most others. There is currently a movement afoot to encourage young people to learn their native tongue. We can only hope for a timely revival of this most important cultural attribute.

Table of Contents

The Intruders   1

The Search   15

The Party   30

The Reveal   49

The Crucible   61

The Murder   75

Cross track   93

The Suspect   112

The Mystery   130

The Investigation   153

The Grind   173

The Reunion   186

The Chase   221

The Fugitive   239

Skullduggery   264

Redemption   287

The Dilemma   298

Glossary   322

1

The Intruders

Arriving early at Legal Services, Chief Investigator Charlie Yazzie sighed as he entered the building, then pulled up short and frowned. Turning to the receptionist's desk, he pointed to the plate-glass window in the back of the room. "What are those two doing in my office, Arlene?"

Looking past the scatter of empty desks the woman raised an eyebrow in surprise. Adjusting her horn-rimmed glasses, she gave a flip of her ponytail. "Beats me boss, maybe someone left the back door unlocked...again." Then in a more defensive tone, "Those two didn't come in past me this morning, that's for damned sure."

He and Arlene watched as the intruders, their backs to the window, appeared to be unrolling a chart, or perhaps a poster. The shorter of the two men steadied a chair for the taller to stand on as he affixed a large piece of artwork to the wall across from the investigator's desk.

Still staring in the direction of the office, Arlene stated flatly, "Chief, this is the second time this month they've gone back there without checking in." Then asked, "Do you want I should call the law?"

The investigator smiled ruefully. "No, we tried that once, remember—turned out to be a bad idea."

Arlene sat back down to her morning report, watching secretly to see if the investigator intended to do anything about this latest infraction of the new security agenda.

Sighing, Charlie started for his private office even as the harried receptionist called after him, "Sir, this is supposed to be a secured area, you know. Something needs to be done about those two!"

Without looking back, Charlie raised a hand as he shook his head. Making his way through the outer desks and entering the office door, he sidled past the two men engrossed in their work. Seating himself at his desk without acknowledging the pair, he nonchalantly busied himself with the latest reports.

Eventually, the trespassers stood back, silently admiring their work. After a long moment, the taller of the two, Thomas Begay, turned to the seated investigator. "After our local fair last night, my daughter dropped off this poster for you at our place. Ida Marie was on her way back home to Cortez and thought it was too late to bother you at home. She did not think it was too late to bother us, I guess. She said we should bring this to your office first thing this morning. For whatever reason, she felt it important you should have it as soon as possible." A snort escaped the man as he turned back to the poster chuckling to himself. "She says you used to know this woman…back in your college days."

Charlie took a deep breath as he looked up at the wall. Leaving his chair without comment, he moved to stand directly in front of the image. The other two men stepped back, leaving him to his thoughts. Each of the three nodded to themselves occasionally as they continued to study the artwork…obviously a promotional poster designed to startle. And as dramatically as possible. The featured woman, unmistakably Indian, appeared pensive under the brim of a bowler hat. But it was the face that held their attention. Masked in stark black and white, the makeup left less than half her features visible. Yet judging by this alone she still would have been quite beautiful. Intense grey eyes suggest mixed blood, her gaze bleak, cat-like, and worldly. Still,

3

one was left with a hidden sense of the inner woman…and even that was unsettling.

The hint of a smile played about the Investigator's lips as he murmured, "Well, our darling Ida Marie does tend to blow things out of proportion now and then, doesn't she?"

Thomas smirked, "I don't raise no wallflowers."

Indicating the image with a lift of his chin, the investigator finally conceded this much: "I did once go to one of her concerts in Albuquerque. She was the warmup for a heavy metal band. I don't remember their name…but I never forgot hers." He chuckled, "Professor Custer had wrangled a stagehand gig for me. The pay was by way of a free concert ticket." Charlie paused momentarily shaking his head. "George Custer, the faculty rabble-rouser, and a major partier back then, took it upon himself to liven up my life." Smiling at the memory, he went on. "After the show, the professor introduced me to this young woman, thinking the two of us, both being Navajo, might have something more in common. We chatted back and forth a while, but it never really went anywhere." He turned to Harley Ponyboy. "And you, Harley. Don't you be talking it around it was anything more—especially not around Sue."

Harley nudged the investigator, as old friends sometimes will, and assured him quietly. "Anything you say, Chief. Anything you say."

Hiding a grin, Thomas Begay nodded to himself. Stroking his chin in a speculative manner, he whispered. "Who'd a' ever guessed... You and Billy Moon...."

Silently gritting his teeth, Charlie was careful not to offer the slightest reaction. *That's what the man is hoping for...but he's not getting it from me today.*

The three remained gazing at the bizarre image for several more minutes when Harley, ever the master of the obvious, commented, "She looks kinda' spooky, huh? Like a *Diné* witch maybe." He touched his tongue to his upper lip and innocently asked, "Did she wear that face paint when you two went out on dates?"

Charlie grimaced, knowing even the slightest attempt at denial would only make things worse. "Not that I recall, she didn't. But, someday, Harley, I'll tell you all about it."

The outer office staff filed into their desks, several casting curious glances at the gathering in the private office. Muted though it might be their banter still could be heard.

Arlene threw a dour glance their way. She'd been here longer than any of the previous receptionists—chiefly because she knew what was best kept to herself—yet even that came at a cost.

Later, as the two intruders were leaving by way of the front door, Charlie grinned as Thomas Begay touched a finger to his lips, and smiled at Arlene, as he raised an eyebrow. The receptionist glared at them as she murmured something under her breath in Navajo.

~~~~~~~

It was nearly noon when Charlie's intercom buzzed as the light flashed intermittently. Arlene, breathless with excitement, came on even as he picked up. "A Ms. Billy Moon is here to see you, sir. Should I send her on back?"

Charlie glanced through the window, a look of surprise crossing his face and said "Yes... Arlene, you may certainly send her back." Taking a deep breath, he studied the near legendary woman as she signed in. The poster, he'd taken off the wall earlier, was now stretched across a chair by the filing cabinet. He glanced from the older woman at the front desk to her image, and then back again, seeing little to indicate they were the same person. Not surprising, considering her current lack of makeup and, of course, the inevitable passage of time. His door stood open, and he mentally braced himself to once again meet the redoubtable Billy Moon.

Her striking grey eyes were first to register. Glossy black hair in a neat braid down her back and plainly dressed in Levi's and a pearl-button western shirt—much as any modern Navajo woman might be wearing these days. Remarkably good-looking for her age—stunningly so, to his way of thinking.

The rock star, recognizing the expression, took the leather chair Charlie indicated, nonchalantly arranging herself with the panache one might expect from one of her celebrity. Even then, Charlie doubted few could have carried it off so well. Settling himself behind the desk with what he hoped was not a starstruck look, he greeted the woman with a smile. "Billy, it's good to see you again."

Silently appraising the man, she nodded amiably enough. 'Well, Charlie, I see what I've heard is true. It appears you have come far here on the *Dinétah,* and, if I may say so, aged well in the process. Lack of stress maybe?"

"Thanks for saying so, Billy. I must admit I'm a little surprised you remember me at all after these many years." then grinning, "And I do suppose the quiet life has been good for me in some ways."

She smiled. "The truth is, Charlie, I probably wouldn't have recalled our last meeting at all, if not for a little chat with your daughter…Ida Marie, is it?"

Charlie laughed outright. "I'm guessing that was my 'goddaughter,' Ida Marie Begay, or rather, I should say Ida Marie Klah, now that she's newly married. I'm her…self-adopted uncle…if you will." Smiling ruefully, he admitted, "Sometime in the past I may have mentioned I'd met you at one of your concerts at UNM. Ida had one of your posters on her wall back then and was, as I recall, a huge fan." Charlie paused a moment, searching for an appropriate way of acknowledging this woman's many achievements without sounding too obsequious. Then in a decidedly more earnest tone, he said, "I'm sure you're aware, Billy, how few 'internationally known' rock stars are from the reservation? The young people out here are, I'm afraid, a little short on heroes. I'm sure you have filled that void for many of them."

Nodding as though she appreciated what he was trying to say, the woman went on, "Ida Marie mentioned your name and who you are, and we chatted for a bit as she brought me up to date. I later signed a poster for her, and, in fact, sent one along for you, as well." Glancing over at the poster, she continued, "I can sign that one, too, if you like?"

"That would please me, Billy. I'm sure my daughter would like to have it for her room." Smiling as before, he continued. "Sasha's my daughter, and while somewhat younger than Ida Marie, she has always wanted to be like her, as much as possible." He hesitated slightly. "By the way, I am sorry I missed your concert last night. To be honest, I wasn't aware you were appearing at our little fair, though I might have expected it at Window Rock or Gallup."

"Ordinarily, I probably wouldn't have been booked here, but I had recently been thinking of coming back for a visit and figured this might be the right time to make that happen. I did see to it there wasn't much in the way of advance publicity." She shrugged. "I like to surprise people."

Charlie took a short breath. "I suspect you've surprised a good many over the years, Billy." And then in a more serious voice asked, "So, you still have relatives hereabouts, do you?"

"Oh, I think I probably do, though some would be quite old by now, and damn me, I haven't kept in touch over the years as I should. There may well be one or two who are already gone." Hesitating a moment, she gave the investigator the impression she wasn't certain how to properly phrase what she was about to say. Finally, raising a finger, which she abruptly dropped, the woman simply came straight out with it. "Charlie, there *is* another reason I'm here, and one I think you might be able to help me with, should you have the time and inclination, of course."

"Oh, and what would that be, Billy? Are you trying to run down someone in particular? I do have contacts among the Tribal agencies, of course I could put out enquiries if you like." Charlie sat back in his chair thinking he saw some flicker of emotion cross the woman's face, but had not the faintest idea what it might mean.

"Ahh…well, yes, running some of those people down has crossed my mind of late. Any help would certainly be appreciated." She laughed shortly. "But what I really had in mind is something a little more pressing even than that."

The Legal Services investigator, cocking his head to one side, studied the woman's face briefly, and judging by her expression, thought she might well have something more serious on her mind.

Billy Moon almost immediately began pouring out the real reason for her visit. "Charlie, what I have to say happened long before your time here at Legal Services and is no reflection on you, of course, but many years ago, when I was still quite young, my father went missing, and later was found dead." She hesitated and started over, "No, we may as well call it what it was…he was found murdered, and not far from where my mother's family lived at the time. As I grow older it seems more and more important for me to know exactly what happened to him…the circumstances of his death. There were family rumors, of course, but all I ever knew for certain was the murder was never solved. I was never given the slightest information or details of his death by anyone in a position of authority. It's only in these last few years I've come to realize knowing might give me the closure I've needed all along. I'm thinking it will take someone with an 'in' of some sort with the FBI, and most likely with Tribal police as well."

Charlie spoke then and in the kindest possible way asked, "Back in that time, Billy, did you voice these concerns of yours to the police or any local authorities?"

"No, I did not, I suppose I was too young and naive then to think that was even possible."

The investigator nodded, agreeing this might well have been difficult at such an age. "The FBI would have been the agency who handled the case, and they should still have records on file regarding the death, at least I would think so."

"I would have thought so, too, Charlie. But despite writing letters and making phone calls, I was never able to speak to anyone who would admit knowing anything about the case. A few years back, when I was finally able to afford it, I did hire a lawyer in Albuquerque, a very expensive lawyer, as it turned out. Still, that never went anywhere, either. I was beginning to suspect the entire thing was being covered up for some reason. That's when I decided to return here to the reservation to see what I could find out locally. Ida Marie caught me for an autograph after the concert, and learning she was related to you, I was inclined to listen when she told me Legal Services would be a good place to start, and that you were the person in charge here." She straightened in her chair and leaned in closer. "Though my father was white, Charlie, my mother was full-blood Navajo, and I am a registered member of the Navajo Nation. Surely, I'm within my rights to ask Legal Services for help," Pausing briefly, she asked, "Is that not so?"

Charlie quickly agreed this was true, yet not wanting to interrupt her train of thought, waited for the woman to continue.

Billy pulled her chair a bit closer, and lowering her voice slightly, whispered, "I'm only asking if there is not some way the case could be reopened, for the sake of the truth, if nothing else." With an audible intake of breath, she looked down at her hands, possibly striving to compose herself. When finally, she glanced back up, it was with misted eyes. Finally finding her voice, she had only one last thing to say. "Should you be able to help me with this, Charlie, I would forever be in your debt."

Taking out a pad and pencil, the investigator quietly began asking those questions he thought relevant to uncovering the information needed. Privately, he thought to himself *this is going to take some digging. It has been a long time since this murder was committed...assuming there actually has been a murder committed.* Records had not always been accurately kept back in that time, and he thought that might prove to be a problem as well. Charlie figured he would eventually find himself at FBI headquarters in Farmington. He knew exactly who to talk to there.

"I believe I have enough information here to make a start, Billy. Are you staying here locally with friends or...?"

"No, actually, my tour bus is still out at the fairgrounds, and I have everything I need there. My driver has been with me for years, and if I'm not there, he will be and can take a message. On the way here, I rented a car in Farmington and intend to poke around a little myself. I'll check in with you from time to time, to see how things are progressing."

The two quickly wrapped up their conversation with Charlie's promise the matter would be looked into as quickly as possible, saying he would probably be getting back to her in a day or so, at the outside.

As the Tribal investigator watched the woman make her way through the outer office, he felt a certain melancholy. Not just for the woman herself but more so for the little girl she once had been. There was something in her plea for help that hinted at some darker thing. Something she perhaps didn't care to make public. On the reservation this might mean a past situation so bottomless she was, even after all these years, unable to admit it, even to herself.

Charlie had been with Legal Services for a number of years now and had heard many a tale of terror and hidden shame. This wouldn't be the first time he had let his work affect him personally. In this instance, however, he had no way of knowing how far off-track Billy Moon's story would take him.

After the woman left the office, he waited a moment then went to the reception area and watched through the front window as she walked out of the building. Her rental turned out to be a luxury Ford SUV, black and brand-new, judging by the paper dealer plate in the rear window, possibly from the Ford dealer rather than an airport rental agency. This told him it was probably a longer-term rental, or even a lease. *Billy Moon may be planning to be here a while*, he thought. It was hard to tell what a woman like this might be thinking. But whatever it was, she was serious about it. Billy Moon had an agenda. It was now clear to him…one way or the other she fully intended to see it through to the end.

2

The Search

Inspector Yazzie was not the sort to let an obligation slide and finding that Billy Moon was indeed enrolled as a member of the Navajo Nation, now felt justified in officially taking up the circumstances of her father's murder—if that was what it was. As a legitimate cold case, he intended pursuing it in a timely fashion. Hopefully in the process, he might discover one or more of her relatives, should there still be any. Finding even one, he thought, might please her, and prove valuable going forward. *Surely there must be someone left that knows something.*

It was only natural then, that his first visit was to his old colleague Fred Smith, once again senior agent for the Farmington Bureau. It had been a long road back for Fred. He had spent a considerable leave of absence recuperating after being seriously wounded in the line of duty. At the time, there were those who doubted he would survive at all. Certainly, no one, including Charlie, had thought they would ever see the man back at his old job. Fred fooled them all. A local boy born and raised, he had an intimate knowledge of the reservation and its people. Growing up with the Navajo from the time he was a youngster and helping summers at his uncle's trading post had given him a certain inside knowledge of the *Diné*. He'd found them fascinating and proved to be a quick study.

Other than not being bullet-proof, Fred had most of the desired qualities required for a senior agent on the reservation. He was smart, tough, and already familiar with the nuances of the culture. Not to mention his genuine fondness for the people of the *Dinétah*. The Bureau knew Agent Fred Smith would be a hard man to replace, and as it turned out, he was.

Charlie and the FBI man were longtime friends whose agencies had cooperated on a number of cases, including the one where they were both shot within moments of each other. Charlie's injuries were not nearly so serious as Fred's, and he was back on the job within weeks. Fred, however, wasn't that lucky…he sustained a life-threatening head injury that after initial surgery, required many months of complicated treatment including ongoing physical therapy before he was able to work his way back to some semblance of his old self and eventually to regain his formal title of "Senior Agent."

Pulling up to the Federal building in Farmington the Investigator found he was, in fact, a few minutes early and spent the time going over a few points he might touch on should Fred prove to be a hard sell. The information he needed was likely hidden right here in this building somewhere, and he meant to find it.

Later, seated in the spacious waiting room, Charlie couldn't help remembering some of his previous meetings here and the close professional ties he'd built with the Bureau these last few years.

At exactly the appointed time, the new secretary glanced up from her work and looking his way announced, "Investigator Yazzie?"

He was ushered into Fred's office where the Agent, already standing, came around the desk and shook his hand. "Long time, Charlie…"

"Yes, yes it has been, but I doubt either of us gets out of the office as much as we used to."

"Isn't that the truth. Have a seat, Charlie." The FBI man smiled, pointing to a plush leather chair in front of his desk. "How's the family? Joseph and Sasha doing well? I shouldn't have to ask—I'm sure Sue's keeping them in line."

Charlie grinned at this. "Oh, everyone at our place is fine…Joseph Wiley is in his first year at the University of New Mexico, and Sasha started High School this term." He smiled inwardly; Fred never neglected the niceties when speaking with a *Diné,* regardless of who it might be. The agent didn't forget family members' names and always observed traditional Navajo protocol in a conversation. Even knowing Charlie wasn't especially traditional himself, it was all the same to him. The Tribal investigator had come to expect this sort of thing from the man and appreciated the effort.

"What brings you into town this morning, Charlie, nothing too grim I hope?"

Cutting directly to the chase the Investigator asked, "Fred, in your time down in Albuquerque, do you remember a rock singer named Billy Moon?"

Fred didn't have to think long. "Oh yes, she was just hitting the charts back then—went on to big things from what I understand. I saw in the paper the other day she was appearing at the local Shiprock fair this week." Fred had a quizzical look on his face, obviously wondering what the rock star might have to do with their meeting this morning—a meeting he had been thinking was no more than a courtesy call.

Charlie smiled wryly. "Well, the woman is in town and came to see me yesterday, asking if Legal

Services could help find out what had happened to her father. *She* maintains he was murdered here on the reservation, back when she was a child. Anything ring a bell there?"

Fred let his chair swivel momentarily to the window. Turning back and shaking his head, he declared. "Not a thing Charlie, I was still a fresh recruit in Albuquerque at the time you are talking about and was working relatively minor stuff." Then admitted, "I wasn't really a fan of hard rock at the time... I'm still not by the way." The senior agent grinned. "I wouldn't have been paying much attention to her I'm afraid. As to this murder thing, you know as well as anyone, there were plenty of murders here on the reservation back then that were never reported...and there still *are* some today."

Charlie agreed with a nod and a sigh. "I get what you're saying, Fred, and I know what I'm asking isn't going to be easy. That's why I didn't make an official request, not as yet anyhow Anything you can do at this stage I would be inclined to consider more of a personal favor."

Fred hesitated only a moment before saying. "Okay, Charlie, you've got it. If you'll leave me what information you have, I'll check into it for you myself. I'll give you a call should I turn up anything."

21

"That works for me, Fred…Oh, and one other thing… Billy Moon's father was white."

Fred raised an eyebrow. "Hmm, well that could make a difference. Not many white deaths go unreported out here, at least not in my experience."

Charlie put the packet of notes he'd prepared on the agent's desk and made his goodbyes. Later, in his Tribal unit down in the parking lot, he picked up the mic and had his office patch him through to Billy Red Clay at Tribal Police. Billy was Liaison Officer between Tribal and the FBI and spent a lot of his time in the field. Charlie wanted to be sure he was in before heading that direction. He didn't want Thomas Begay's nephew to think he was going around him in this. He had mentored the young officer as he worked his way up the ladder and wasn't inclined to put that relationship at risk.

~~~~~~~

Billy Red Clay was not in his office, but was, as he said, on his way back to Shiprock by way of *Beklabito* and was going to stop in for some lunch at the *Diné Bikeyah* cafe. He set a time and Charlie agreed to meet him there. It reminded him he was hungry, too.

When the investigator pulled in, he spotted Billy's patrol unit parked right up front. The lunch crowd had already thinned, leaving plenty of room in the parking lot to maneuver, which was not always the case. It was a popular place in that sparsely peopled area. Still, this time of day, there should be a good chance they'd have their choice of a table. The law enforcement crowd had a long-established preference for the back corner table by the window. It offered the most privacy and the best view of the front door. Local law officers were well known to the employees, especially the waitresses, who knew which table they preferred, and wouldn't seat anyone else there unless there was no other choice. The table was known as the "cop-shop" to the regulars, and most avoided it when possible.

Sure enough, as soon as he walked through the door, he saw the Tribal policeman waving from the coveted table. As Charlie came up, Billy kicked a chair out for him and rose to shake hands. "How go's it, Kemo Sabe?"

Charlie was too tired to buy into this opening gambit. "How's your mom, Billy?"

"Ahh, she's fine. What about your crew, everything okay out there in the suburbs?"

Before the investigator could answer, the younger man came back with, "Guess what? I moved out of my mom's place and got an apartment over in Government Housing. And you'll never guess which unit it is!"

Charlie didn't have to think about it. "My old apartment, right?"

"Uh…that's right, how'd you know?"

"The manager over there called my office for a reference."

"Really? Man…really?" Billy Red Clay was astonished, "They check out a *cop*'s references?"

"They *especially* check out cop's references, Billy. You guys are well known for loud parties, breaking up furniture…and well…a lot of other things."

Billy's eyes widened. "Geeze, Charlie, I never knew that. No one at Tribal ever invited me to any parties." He was quick to admit, "The management did just paint and re-do everything over there, but still, I never figured they would check *me* out like this."

Unable to hold a straight face any longer, Charlie busted out laughing. "I'm just messing with you, *Hastiin.* No one called my office. Our receptionist Arlene has a place over there now and said she saw you moving in. She knew it was my old place. She did say it looked like you had a girlfriend helping you—what's up with that?"

The young cop puffed up. "For your information, wise guy, that wasn't my girlfriend, she's, my cousin.

24

You know her, she lives right out there by you and Harley. Jeannie Johnson, her dad has that place back behind Harley Ponyboy's little ranchito. Geeze, how long have you lived out there... A long time I know."

"Johnsons? Never heard of them."

"Okay, now you're putting me on again." Billy Red Clay was accustomed to taking anything Charlie Yazzie said at face value and was not used to this sort of teasing from the investigator.

Charlie made a long face. "I'm sorry, Billy, I don't know what got into me." Then grinning, said, "Maybe I'm hanging out with your Uncle Thomas too much."

"Okay! Okay, seriously now what was on your mind that was important enough to spoil my lunch?"

"You know who Billy Moon is, don't you?"

"Everyone on the Res knows who Billy Moon is." He looked the investigator in the eye. "I just saw her last night...at the fair, I mean...cops in uniform get in for free at those concerts. I guess the promoters never know when they might need them."

"Any trouble?"

"Nope, everything went slick as goose grease. I saw my cousin Ida out there, though...She had a couple of Billy Moon Posters under her arm. I would have liked to have had one, but she said they were already spoken for. Of course, they were sold out by the time I got out there. The signed ones are pricey, too. I don't know where people get their money these days."

Charlie was nodding his head at all this. "How would you like me to get you one for free, pardner, and a signed one, at that?"

"For free? Uncle Thomas must have been right, about you and her being lovers, huh?"

"Forget about anything your Uncle Thomas says. Okay? And that goes for Harley Ponyboy, too."

Billy chuckled. "He didn't really say that. I was just messing with you."

Charlie lifted his gaze toward the ceiling. "Listen, Billy, I need you to do something for me." He waited for the nod. "See what you can turn up on Billy Moon. Who her relatives are and anything you can find in Tribal files about the death of her father back when she was a kid. There may be something in the files or you may just have to ask around. Uh…and I need it as soon as possible too if you have time." Charlie grinned. "That poster will be waiting for you at my office."

Nodding his head, Billy looked up, "Here comes Irene, the new waitress. She's something, isn't she?"

Charlie looked that way. "What happened to the old Irene?"

"Got married and moved away from what I hear. But unlike the other one, I think this Irene actually likes me."

Seeing the new Irene snag a fresh pot as she passed the station, the pair hurriedly flipped their cups upright.

"So, how're you guys today?" Not waiting for an answer, she filled their cups and set the steaming pot on the table. She bumped the young Officer on the shoulder. "Where you been, Billy? You haven't been in here in a while." She said this with a sad little pout that made the cop smile.

"Work, work, work…nice to hear you missed me, though." Looking over to see Charlie's arched eyebrow, Billy turned red around the collar and began fiddling with his coffee.

After Irene took their orders and started for the kitchen, the men doctored their coffee as Billy Red Clay stared after her. "Pretty girl, huh?"

"Yes, I'd say so." There was no denying it. Something about the girl bothered him though, some poignant nostalgia, not a memory exactly, more like the ghost of one flickered through his mind like a silent film clip.

Billy chattered on like a magpie who'd found a shiny marble. "I went to high school with her, she was only a couple of grades below me."

Charlie turned to look after the girl. "She does look familiar for some reason; I just can't seem to place her, that's all."

"She comes from over around Crown Point where we used to live when I was a kid." Billy followed the new girl with his eyes as she turned in their orders and sat back in his chair. Then, as if recalling the thread of their conversation, he answered, "Right, Charlie, I have to go over to my mom's place to pick up the last of my stuff tonight. I'll ask her if she knows anything about Billy Moon. We lived over in that area for years. There's a chance she might have known some of that bunch back then. Even at her age she don't forget much."

Charlie had a strange sensation he had missed something. "I didn't know Billy Moon was from over there. For some reason, I always thought she came from right here in Shiprock." He studied the ceiling a moment thinking something might come to him…but it didn't. Moving past the lost thought the investigator went on. "Oh, I did want to tell you I saw Fred Smith this morning and asked him to check the Bureau files for me if he got a chance—just so you'll be in the loop. You know."

Billy bobbed his head, but he was watching Irene again, his mind clearly somewhere else.

Charlie nodded as he picked up the check. "Between the three of us, I'm sure we will turn up something."

Billy Red Clay beamed—it wasn't that often someone bought his lunch. "Thanks, Charlie, I'll catch you next time." Again, looking across the room at the waitress he whispered, "I'll leave a little something extra for Irene. She works really hard here, you know, and they don't pay a whole lot." Digging in his pocket he pulled out a surprisingly generous tip which he set under the edge of his plate.

As Charlie paid the tab at the front counter, he noticed Billy stopping to have a last word with Irene at the coffee station. He doubted the young officer had even heard what he'd said about seeing Agent Smith. Ah, well, he'd been young once himself, though it seemed like a long time ago now.

Outside, the investigator, looked up at an overcast sky. Some weather had moved in over the last few hours, as it so often did in that country. *I'll bet there's a pretty good size system making up on the plateau. Fall is probably about done,* he thought sadly. He couldn't help wondering if his aunt, Annie Eagletree, had started moving her cows down off the Carrizos. Bad weather came without warning at that altitude. Thomas and Harley generally gathered stock for Annie each year. He'd have to ask if she'd called them about that yet. He didn't know what his aunt would do without him or his friends to help out this time of year. The three of them had been up there only last month making sure she had a healthy supply of firewood on hand. It was his opinion this winter would be a long and cold one. But fuel for the wood-stove would not be something his aunt would have to worry about.

3

The Party

Driving home from work that evening Charlie stopped for milk and bread. He'd almost forgotten Sue had called to leave the message.

"Don't forget it," she'd said with a hint of irony. "There won't be much of a supper without it."

He had to think about that a second or two. He' told her he wouldn't forget, and he didn't. Now, if only he could remember where he'd seen that waitress Irene from lunch at the *Diné Bikeyah*. His memory wasn't what it used to be, and this bothered him. He wondered if he'd ever seen her before, or not. There was something there, for sure.

Billy Red Clay was attracted to the girl, and that wasn't hard to understand. A good thing in his opinion. Billy had had several girlfriends over the years, but nothing long term as far as Charlie could see. The young man was a good person and a fine police officer, too. His only fault, according to several former girlfriends, was his total dedication to his job. That's the way it had been since he started on the force, becoming even more noticeable after he made Liaison Officer to the FBI. Maybe now that was about to change. Irene seemed like a nice girl, and a very pretty one as well. He wondered if Billy had asked about Clan affiliation. That would be the next step for someone from a traditional background. Of course, like most young people, the old ways didn't seem quite as important as they once had.

Charlie, himself, had been away at school for a long time and now was not very traditional himself. At times he regretted this, especially back when Old Man Paul T'Sosi was alive. The Singer had constantly encouraged him to become more grounded in the old ways. Now that Paul was gone, however, Charlie again found himself drifting ever further from his people's customs.

When Charlie and his wife first became a couple, it was Sue who made sure those stars aligned in their proper order. He felt fortunate they had been so lucky.

Most were aware how such ancient taboos originated, and why. From the earliest days of the *Diné* it was forbidden for people with closely related Clan ties to be together. Even back in ancient times the dangers of inbreeding were well understood…and strictly forbidden.

This was true of many if not all tribes, but the *Diné* seemed to carry it to a higher level than some. Still, Charlie reasoned, things were different now, the gene pool was vastly larger and much more diversified than it was in ancient times. Yet, in the back of his mind, he knew when his own children's time came to choose a mate, he would want to have a little peek at their Clan affiliations before things went too far.

~~~~~~~

Pulling up to his mailbox in the amber glow of a slow setting sun, the investigator glanced up the hill toward Harley Ponyboy's place, only to see the man and his son coming down the drive at a hurried pace. Charlie could see the boy was talking a mile a minute, gesturing with his hands as if to explain something to his father. Charlie shook his head as they came closer—the boy was already half as tall as Harley and showed promise of someday being much taller. He had matured considerably these last couple of years, becoming more amiable, more secure possibly. Knowing the conditions his father had rescued him from as a toddler, Charlie was surprised how far he had come. Harley had been a wonderful parent over the years, but his new wife had figured into it in a major way as well. It was a real mother the boy had needed, and Celia had proven to be the right one.

As the father and son drew closer the boy finally looked up from his non-stop chatter and noticed his "adopted Uncle" at the mailbox. With a joyful grin young Harley broke into a ground-eating sprint. He hadn't seen Charlie in several days and was doubtless anxious to tell him the same story he'd been telling his father.

Charlie held up a cautionary hand to slow him down and called, "Whoa!" as the boy skidded to a stop in front of him. "What's the hurry, big boy? You almost ran over your poor old uncle." The investigator grinned as he said this, but the boy knew he was serious just the same. "Now then, tell me what's so exciting."

It took the boy only a moment to catch his breath. "Well…my new horse Dad bought me… tried to buck me off again. But this time, I stayed on 'til he quit and settled down." He looked up at Charlie. "I think I learned him a good lesson this time."

Charlie gave him a surprised look. "Wow! How many jumps did he make?"

"I don't know. I guess I kinda' lost count, but it was a lot…I didn't think he would ever stop!"

"Well, that's just fine Harley, I'll bet your dad is proud of you, too."

"Yes, I am." The boy's father hurried up, appearing nearly as excited as his son. "You should have seen it, Charlie, I was standing right there when the horse blew up on him, and he handled it like a pro. Why, I doubt even I could of have done any better."

Charlie laughed at this. "Well, like father, like son, I guess."

The two Harleys beamed back, equally pleased, and more than a little proud. Then the elder Harley frowned for a second. "I hope you remembered the milk and bread. Sue invited us for dinner tonight but said she might have to take it back if you forgot."

Charlie jerked a thumb at his truck, chuckling, "I got 'em all right., So, I guess it's still on. What's for dinner?"

"Those girls would not say a word about it, but Celia and Sue have been cooking up a storm for a while now, and things are starting to smell pretty good up there. Your Aunt Annie dropped off a package this morning, and I expect it has something to do with dinner, too." Harley licked his lips. "I got a feeling it's going to be something extra good. I'm not sure, but I think Thomas and Lucy Tallwoman are coming too." He turned to go with little Harley right behind him, when he stopped and looked back. "Oh, I almost forgot. We'll be eating up at our place, just more room, I guess. Take your time, it'll probably be a while before everything's ready.

Back in his truck, Charlie sat a moment as the father and son trundled up the drive to their house. *It's funny Sue didn't mention them going up to the Ponyboy's for dinner.* He had a feeling he wouldn't have known any of this if he hadn't run into these two at the mailbox. *Ah well...* where women were concerned, he had never been a good guesser.

~~~~~~

Coming through the front door, Charlie glanced through the living room to the kitchen as Sasha and her mother stood at the kitchen sink, their heads close together as they laughed over their work. *Those two are nearly the same height now. How did I not notice that before. They've always looked alike,"* he thought, *"Sasha is going to be as pretty as her mother...from the back they could be sisters.* As he shut the door, the pair turned in surprise.

"Hey, got the stuff?" Sue called.

He lifted the grocery bag for them to see. "Why do we need a gallon of milk? Won't this go bad before we use all of it? Your son's not here to slurp it up, you know."

"Oh, I know. We'll use it, don't you worry about that."

Charlie set the bag on the counter and stepped back out of the way. Dishes of food sat everywhere, hot out of the oven, and all of it smelled great. Over the years, Sue had spent a lot of time learning how to cook, mostly from her Home ec classes in boarding school. Eventually, she had become quite good at it. She did a good job on the more traditional dishes, too. Just the thought of it was making him hungry. "So, anything I can do to help you two?"

"You're doing it—just stand aside and let the magic happen." Sue sounded happier than she had in days.

Sasha, shaking her head, shooshed him out of the room saying, "Just go get cleaned up, Dad. We're going to take all this stuff up to Celia's place and finish it out up there."

Sue turned and looked at him. "You look tired, Charlie, you've got plenty of time for a hot shower. Everything will be ready by the time you get there."

His daughter pointed toward the door, "There's a cooler on the front porch… Could you load that up and bring it with you? Your Aunt Annie brought us a little dinner gift this morning."

"I can do that." The fact was a hot shower sounded good to him about now. The Billy Moon thing had taken up his entire day. It had been hectic from the get-go, and that sort of stress always caused a muscle in his neck to knot up. *And now, something else is going on.* He could see that, now, and would just have to deal with it as it came.

~~~~~~

Sue had been right; the shower was just what he'd needed. He put on the fresh shirt and Levi's she had laid out for him, and then took a quick swipe or two at the dust on his boots with the damp towel before hiding it in the clothes basket. He didn't know what was going on up at the Ponyboys, but he figured to be on his game when he walked into it.

Outside the front door, he hefted the cooler a time or two before deciding to put it in the back of the truck. He'd just drive it up there. *No need to get all sweated up before dinner.* He didn't even take the Chevy out of reverse—backing it up nearly to Harley's porch with the tailgate down. Stepping down from the truck he noticed several cars and pickups parked along the shared drive. Some he knew and some he didn't. He set the cooler by the steps and rang the doorbell. Almost immediately all the lights inside dimmed.

It hit him then. *Ahh, crap, it's my birthday.* Like many Navajo of his era, his family never paid much attention to birthdays. Through the years he and Sue hadn't made a big deal of it, either. Their kids got a cake and a small present on their birthday, and he generally took his wife out to dinner on her day. But that was about it. When Charlie's turn came Sue would make him a nice meal at home, and there would be a comic greeting card letting him know how far along he was. There had never been a party.

The door flung open, and little Harley stood there with a huge grin on his face. Everyone in the room yelled, "Surprise!" and began singing Happy Birthday as the lights went up. Charlie was dumbfounded when Billy Moon stepped forward and belted out the chorus.

Heat rose to his face, and when the rock star finished her contribution with a professional flourish, everyone cheered and clapped for several minutes. He couldn't remember when he'd been more embarrassed.

Sue took his hand, leading him into the dining room which displayed the obligatory number of balloons along with a huge banner strung across one wall. HAPPY 40TH BIRTHDAY in sparkling scarlet letters. Charlie's knees nearly buckled, and he felt a little weak as he squeezed Sue's hand to steady himself. *That's it... everyone knows I'm 40 years old now.* He'd been dreading this day for a couple of years but was always able to put it out of his mind, so much so, he hadn't even remembered it himself.

He lifted his hands to the crowd and as calmly as possible declared, "I really don't know what to say..."

Instantly there were wild cheers and more applause from the crowd, who evidently thought a lawyer not knowing what to say was hilarious...leading Charlie to believe he'd said enough.

Sue seated her husband at the middle of the long narrow table—allowing everyone a fair shot at him, she said. The others filled in around him in no particular order, Billy Moon directly across the table. Harley Ponyboy to his left along with the other Harley, and an empty chair for the boy's stepmother. To his right was Charlie's daughter and an empty chair for *her* mother, as well.

Thomas Begay and his wife Lucy Tallwoman were seated on the other side of the table, to the left of

Billy Moon. And on her right was Billy Red Clay. Charlie noticed several other places had settings as well and wondered if someone else was coming…or possibly had been invited but were not coming?

At the last moment a knock came at the door, which Charlie intuitively guessed might be his Aunt Annie Eagletree. He doubted she had ever used a doorbell in her life, though it had been pointed out to her on several occasions. Annie preferred the certainty of knocking, which she maintained offered a more personal indicator of who was outside. In this instance that had proven to be true.

Little Harley ran to open the door, and Annie came in, going immediately to her nephew, and giving him a peck on the cheek. A quick hug and she made her way to the head of table and seated herself, as was her right.

Sue and Celia began filling water glasses and setting small plastic champagne glasses beside each plate. They had worked for a week planning this surprise dinner party, going so far as to check out the library's only two volumes on the subject. The books were already several years old but had never been taken out until now. The subject of formal dinner parties was covered in some depth, still, a good amount of improvising was required to fit the current set of circumstances. The two women had both attended functions where alcohol was offered, and it may have been these memories which convinced them to regulate the supply.

Just as they were preparing for the birthday toast, the last guest arrived. The fashionably late Professor George Armstrong Custer was no novice when it came to parties and would not have missed this one for anything. Ignoring the doorbell, he didn't bother knocking either—simply came through the door with arms held wide in greeting.

George knew everyone there and was not intimidated in the least. Waving at the happy gathering, he immediately spotted Billy Moon and called, "Long time Billy... Loved the concert last night." So, saying, he blew the woman a kiss. Then going directly to the empty space at the other end of the table, he seated himself as an elder which, in a manner of speaking, he was. Unfolding his napkin, he caught Charlie's eye and winked.

Sue leaned down to her husband and whispered, "I thought you said he'd quit drinking."

Charlie glanced down-table at his old friend and mentor. "He may just be putting on an act, joking maybe. Harley says he does that sometimes. *He* finds it amusing."

Unconvinced, Sue nodded as she shook her head, "I guess we'll see, won't we?"

Celia came with two champagne bottles from the cooler and passed one to Sue. "Are we serving everyone?"

"Everyone but the kids," She replied."

Raising her eyebrows toward the end of the table Celia whispered, "George must already have had a few?"

"Oh, Charlie thinks he's only putting on an act."

Celia watched him for a moment longer, nodding thoughtfully. "Well, he plays a good part."

When all the glasses were filled, it was George Custer who stood to give the toast. Whether he had been chosen for the job or had just taken it upon himself was irrelevant. The professor held up his glass, and in his most sonorous tone launched into an account of Charlie's notable accomplishments at UNM, including those under his own tutelage. He then briefly covered the man's progression through the ranks at Legal Services. "My only regret, is that I was never able to convince Charlie to change his studies from law to archaeology, or at the least anthropology." George had delivered many such addresses and had a genius for an audience's attention span. Clearly, he felt now was a good time to wrap things up. "We, his relatives and closest friends, have gathered here tonight not only to honor Charlie's past accomplishments but to offer our heartfelt wishes

43

for an ever-brighter future." Raising his glass he announced, "Here's to Charlie Yazzie on his 40th birthday!" And then, nodding to the birthday boy, offered this parting gem of wisdom. "It is a scientific fact," he announced, "that people who have more birthdays…live longer." With that Dr. Custer held his glass high, and everyone drank to the guest of honor. A long and boisterous applause followed…including a couple of wolf whistles from his Aunt Annie Eagletree.

Sue and Celia led a procession of women to the kitchen to bring in the platters of food still hot from the ovens, including the two standing-rib roasts supplied by Charlie's Aunt Annie—along with other delectable dishes of a like nature.

Later, the entire party agreed it to be one of their finest dining experiences—ever. Coffee was served in the living room, allowing people to chat with one another as they cast covert glances at the party's most illustrious guest. Thanks to both Billy Moon and George Custer's efforts to liven things up, the after-dinner conversation was both plentiful and lively. As Sue filled Charlie's glass for the second time, he whispered, "Who, by the way, invited Billy Moon? Not that it's a problem, of course, just wondering."

"I did." Sue studied his face as she spoke. "When I called to invite George this morning, he mentioned

Billy was in town and an old acquaintance of yours. We thought she might add a little life to the party. That's not embarrassing you, is it?"

"No, not at all," he lied, "It's just that I'm currently looking into the death of her father here on the reservation—but there was no way you, or George, could have known that at the time. In any case...no harm done... None at all."

Sue appeared thoughtful for a moment and then smiled. "Did you actually date her in college?"

Giving a deep sigh Charlie looked up slightly, rotating his head side to side like a boxer trying to ward off a twist of nerves before a big bout. "Harley tell you that?"

"No, Ida Marie called this morning to wish you a happy birthday. She said some little something that led me to believe you might have dated her." She shrugged. "That was all a long time ago.... It really doesn't matter," She looked past him, and he turned to see Celia beckoning her. Sue walked away looking quite satisfied with herself.

Charlie stood there a moment thinking this over. *You're damned right it was a long time ago. And it never happened, neither.*

Billy Red Clay edged up beside him. "Happy birthday, big guy!" He was still swirling the remnants of champagne in his glass.

"Are you going to drink that?"

"No, you know I don't drink, but I did take a little sip for the toast. I didn't like it…I'm glad I don't drink."

Charlie reached out. "Well, let me have it then," and tossed it off in a single gulp. "Ah, good stuff," he said cringing slightly.

Billy raised an eyebrow but nodded. "Fred Smith called just as I was leaving the office. He said he was sorry, but something had come up and he wouldn't be able to make the party tonight. He did say he had something for you on the Moon case. I have to go by his office in the morning anyway—I can drop it off on my way back, if you want?"

"That would be fine, Billy," Charlie had a faraway look in his eye. "That would be great." He turned away and walked over to Celia Ponyboy. "Any of that bubbly left, Celia?"

She looked surprised, but said, "Not much, Charlie, a couple drinks maybe…You want me to get it for you?"

"Oh, no, I see the bottles in there by the sink, I'll get it myself, thank you."

Harley came up as the investigator was walking away. His wife told him what was going on and he laughed. "I looked at how much was left after the toast... It's not enough to get a pissant drunk."

"Harley, it's not even real champagne, it's some kind of imitation stuff. I'm just wondering, that's all. I've never seen Charlie drink anything before."

"Maybe he knows it's not real. He don't drink...I know that." The pair sidled over and peeked into the kitchen just as Billy Moon came by taking an armful of dirty dishes to the sink. The rock star smiled at the couple in passing and Celia nodded politely in returned.

The pair stared after the woman, interested to see what might come from this chance meeting. "She seems nice enough to me," Celia said thoughtfully.

Harley chuckled. "You think everyone is nice, Celia." Dropping his voice, he added secretively, "There's something wrong about her—Thomas thinks so, too—we can't figure out exactly what it is, but it's there."

Celia put a hand on her hip and cocked her head to one side, "Really. Something's wrong with her? Neither one of you has ever been off the reservation for more than a day or two at a time. The woman's an international star, for God's sake, been all over the world. She's rich, more than anyone we know. I think you and Thomas better rethink this...that's what I think. It's not everyday people like me and you get to hang out with someone like her."

Harley had never heard his wife use this tone with him and didn't quite know what to make of it. He tried to think of something to say but only stood biting his lip and watching as she walked away. It was alarming somehow.

In the kitchen, Charlie was just filling his glass for the second time, and turned to smile at Billy Moon as she sashayed in. "Can I pour you another little drink?" he asked, holding up the bottle."

"Nope, no thank you, I don't drink that stuff."

"You don't drink champagne?"

"Oh, I drink champagne, all right. But that's not champagne. You knew that didn't you?"

Charlie lifted the bottle to the light, reading the label. Sobering instantly, he murmured, "Well, I'll just be damned. I had no idea."

Billy laughed. "Well, I guess if you don't drink, you don't know." She gave him an odd look, "Really, you didn't drink in college?"

"Oh, a beer now and then with the guys... Not much."

Unloading the dishes, Billy turned and for a moment looked as though she might leave it at that, then apparently changing her mind, said, "I've been around drunks all my life, Charlie. From the time I was little, till this very day. And even knowing better, I'll still go on a little drinking jag myself, now and then. Not often, you know, but now and then." She glanced over at him. "Sometimes things just start piling up on a person, if you know what I mean?"

Charlie nodded. He'd seen it many times himself and had a pretty good idea what she meant. He shifted his weight from foot to foot and, clearing his throat, he changed the subject. "Billy, the FBI has something for us…about your father. We'll know more in the morning." He felt remarkably sober now, glancing around the room to make certain no one saw, a grin erupted as he poured the dregs down the drain.

4

The Reveal

The following morning Billy, Red Clay arrived at Legal Services early. Finding no one at the reception desk and being a law officer, he went straight back to Charlie's office without fear of recrimination.

The investigator had made sure he was there equally early and grinned at the policeman, "How are you this morning, Billy? Not too hungover I hope." He chuckled, but not for long.

"No, I guess I must be getting better at holding my liquor." The Tribal officer laid a folder on the desk. "Agent Smith was anxious to get back to a conference call when I came by his office and didn't say what's in this. But he did seem pleased as he passed it over. I took that to mean it's something significant." Clearly, Billy felt he should be brought up to date on the matter. He was liaison officer to the FBI, and in his view, that had to mean something.

Charlie picked up the file, the cover marked "Confidential," and placed it to one side. "I appreciate you bringing this by, Billy. After I go over the morning reports, I'll take a look at it, and if there's anything I think you can use in here, I'll see that you get a copy."

Billy averted his gaze for a moment then sighed and went on to another matter. "Charlie, I did come by some information myself this morning. Some of it you may already know, but I'll leave this with you anyway."

The officer cleared his throat as he glanced over at the coveted rock star poster sitting next to the filing cabinet. "My mom remembered some of those people living outside Crown Point. This was when Billy Moon was a young child. Mom had apparently met Billy's father at some point—you knew he was white—didn't you?"

The investigator nodded. "She told me so, herself. I mentioned it to Fred Smith when I went to see him yesterday morning. He seemed to think it might make things easier when it came to finding some record of the man."

"Well, anyway, my mom said he was always very nice to everyone around there, even if he was white. The couple lived in a trailer-house over near her mother's

51

family. And you know how some of those people are around there, well, my mom says they were even worse back then—all the time blaming any kind of misfortune on curses or witches and that sort of thing. They thought grey eyes were a bad sign, too, you know. They called them Skinwalker eyes. When her parents had Billy, she had the grey eyes just like her father. Well, that's when they started being a little mean to her... Billy, I mean, they wouldn't let her play with her cousins or come around their place for a long time."

Charlie shook his head. "How did her father, Wayne Moon, make a living? There wasn't much going on out there at the time from what I've heard."

The policeman frowned as he remembered what his mother had said. "Supposedly, he had been a missionary teacher of some kind, but when his wife, Polly, died, mom said he turned away from religion altogether. Still, he always seemed to have a little money and was generous with it. That was why the family tolerated him as long as they did. After Billy Moon's mother died though, they started blaming him for that too, saying he'd put a curse on her. It was only a few days after his disappearance that he was found dead along a back-country road. Being mid-winter and bitterly cold, some assumed he just died of exposure. That's when the Navajo relatives took the little girl in... tried to make a real

Diné out of her…even paid for an expensive cleansing ceremony. But it didn't seem to help according to them. That's when the beatings began…and a lot worse, too."

Charlie sat a minute, trying to reconcile this in his mind. The traditional Navajo did not generally mistreat children in any way. "Did your mother happen to mention the family's name?"

"I was just getting to that. It was Kly. The uncle's name was Rupert Kly, and his wife was Rosemary. They had three children of their own, but my mom couldn't remember their names. One of them, a boy, died when he was still young. She never heard what became of the other two…both girls, as she recalled."

The investigator wrote the names down in his notebook then came around the desk. Picking up the Billy Moon poster, he handed it over to the policeman, who smiled his thanks as he ran a finger across the signature, then held it gingerly by the edges to avoid creasing it.

The office staff was settling into their morning routine, as was Arlene at the front desk. Charlie watched through his office window as the departing Billy Red Clay spoke with the receptionist. He appeared to be showing her the poster, and both were still smiling as he left. Arlene obviously liked the young officer, and Charlie guessed she might be thinking she would be seeing

53

more of him, now that they lived in the same neighbor-hood.

Charlie turned his attention to the sealed manila envelope from Agent Smith. Cutting it open with his penknife, he laid the papers out on his desk. A handwritten note was clipped to the top of the first packet. Fred wanted him to know his investigation was ongoing, and there should be more to come within a day or so.

The investigator leafed through the material, thinking it already more than he'd expected this soon. The coroner's report was on top, only two pages, which he thought was about right for back in that time. In those day's some Navajo deaths on the reservation were never investigated, or even reported. Being white had apparently made the difference in the case of Wayne Moon.

On the second page under Cause of Death it noted simply "Undetermined." *That's strange,* Charlie thought to himself. He turned back to the first page and looked at the date—Feb 15th. According to the report the weather was bitterly cold when the body was found. The remains were discovered within a day or so of death. *The body should have been in good enough condition for a thorough evaluation. Odd, there was no cause of death listed.*

The medical examiner's name was on the certificate, and Charlie wrote it down. He doubted the man was still alive. Coroners were generally older or retired doctors back then, but he intended to check on this, nonetheless. He laid the death certificate aside and turned to an old xerox copy of the original Tribal investigator's report written by one Officer Robert Hoskinny, an experienced patrolman. Hoskinny proved to be a very thorough investigator, even confirming the names of the Navajo family who were Moon's in-laws. He'd also made note of local reports of alleged abuses committed by Rupert Kly against certain family members. Robert too, mentioned the weather being quite cold.

Fred's packet also contained a brief report pulled from the Bureau's files to the effect that Rupert Kly had a long record of assault and other alleged charges. Yet the man seemed to have a remarkable ability to slip past these legal problems with little more than minor consequences. *This Rupert Kly may have had some sort of connections. Nepotism and outright graft were not uncommon back then, even at the highest levels.*

There were no currently known addresses on file for any of the Kly family. They had reported Billy Moon as a runaway a year or so after her father's death. Charlie was still mulling over these last reports when his intercom flashed a call. Instinctively, he glanced through the office window to Arlene's desk and saw it was Billy Moon herself chatting with the receptionist. Staring down at the intercom he wondered what had become of the buzzer. *Always something,* he thought as he signaled Arlene to send the woman back.

Charlie was putting away the files as Billy came through the door. As she seated herself in front of the desk, he couldn't help thinking there was a difference somehow in the way she carried herself. She was dressed much as she had been the visit before, but there seemed to be a calmer and more assured bearing about the woman that he found interesting.

"Great birthday dinner Charlie. I haven't had so nice a time since…Well, I don't know when. I think it did me good to be around my people again."

"Glad to hear it, Billy. I know everyone there enjoyed meeting you and everyone was impressed with how at ease you were among us regular people."

Laughing, Billy exclaimed, "Good to know I can still pass for one of the gang. I sometimes worry I might have lost that ability."

He smiled at the woman. "Well, that doesn't appear to be happening, not from what I've seen anyway. Seems to me you still fit in."

"I wasn't aware the *Diné* gave dinner parties. They certainly didn't, back in my time on the Res."

Charlie smiled. "I must admit it was a first for us, too. In fact, I think I can safely say, no one there had ever attended one like it—barbeques and cookouts, yes, but nothing so upscale as what you saw last night. My wife's doing, for the most part, though apparently just about everyone had a hand in it. Now, most of them think we should do it more often."

"I can't think why they wouldn't. In my few days back, it's clear from what I've seen that the *Diné* are moving ahead, not just to a different lifestyle, but an altogether different way of thinking. I wouldn't have thought it possible back when I was living out here."

"There is no doubt change is coming, Billy, and much of it due to our women. Lucy Tallwoman, who you met last night—on the Tribal council—as are several other women. That would have been rare when I was young. There can be no doubt it's been good for the Navajo Nation. We have been a matrilineal society for eons. Still, for most it will be a slow process—this coming back to center."

Billy Moon smiled grimly, "The mills of the Gods grind slowly…huh Charlie?"

The investigator shrugged and paraphrased, "Yet they grind exceeding fine." He hadn't expected Longfellow, but it would be the rare lawyer who didn't know these words. He pushed the FBI report her way and sat back to study her face as she read. Her jaw clinched as she reviewed the death certificate and her grey eyes turned to ice as she came to the report of Officer Hoskinny. Charlie could only imagine what she must be thinking. Whatever it was, he felt he might be better off not knowing.

When finally, Billy finished the entire report, she flipped back through a few pages, re-read a line or two, and then pushed the papers back across to him. The two stayed staring at one another, not saying anything, each with their own thoughts.

When Billy Moon did speak, it was nearly a whisper, emotionless and without a trace of rancor. "You and I are different from most out here, aren't we Charlie? Not from one another, but from our own people. We were escapees, weren't we? You by hard work and a good and calculated education. Me by some luck of the draw coupled with a glimmer of talent and a hell of a lot of hard work."

Charlie got up from his chair, moving to the window overlooking the parking lot, and then shooting a glance beyond that to the twin towers of the power plant on the banks of the San Juan. And in the far distance, the misty image of the great Shiprock. "How old were you when you left the reservation, Billy?"

"I was sixteen years old when I finally ran away. I don't think anyone ever looked for me, at least not that I was aware of."

"That must have been tough."

"You'll never know how tough, but it still was better than what I'd left behind."

Charlie smiled at her. "I can see by your expression you don't understand why I would come back here after college, do you? You think I'm one of those back-to-the-blanket *Diné* who can't break free of the reservation—even with a golden opportunity laid out before me. It would seem so, wouldn't it? I don't blame you for thinking that, why wouldn't you?"

Billy sighed. "No, Charlie, I don't think any of those things about you. And there is that other little difference between the two of us. I am only half *Diné*... Yes, I know what they say, if your mother is Navajo then you are Navajo, and everyone must accept you as such. That's not always true, not in my experience it isn't. Maybe it is for some... But the opposite certainly isn't true, is it? No. When you are living in the white world you are only half-white, a half-breed, and for most that means you have no people."

Charlie nodded slowly. The truth was the truth and there was little else to be said for it.

The woman reached over and tapped a finger on the report. "What does 'Undetermined' mean, exactly, Charlie—that they could not figure out what happened, or the cause of death?" There was a catch in her voice as she stood and turned away for a moment to collect herself.

Charlie was deliberately serious when he said, "Billy, there is one thing I want you to know. I will not let this go until I have an answer for you. I will press the Bureau, and Tribal, to open their own official investigations into the circumstances of your father's death. With what has already been learned, I don't see how they can avoid it."

"Are you sure that's all that can be done?"

"No, I'm not, I am undertaking my own inquiry, as well. I can promise you I will do everything in my power to help you." Secretly, Charlie was thinking, *there is still a lot this woman hasn't said. Understandable given the circumstances, but some of those things will have to come out before we go much beyond this. I wonder if she knows that.*

Billy Moon looked him directly in the eye for a moment and then standing, without saying anything further, she turned and left the office.

Charlie stared after her, interoffice workers followed her with hooded eyes, as she breezed past Arlene's desk. Nibbling at his upper lip he thought. *She's not going to leave this to the law…not now, she isn't.*

~~~~~~

Glancing at the wall clock Charlie noted the time: 11:30 AM and he was hungry. What to do for lunch? That was the immediate question. The intercom buzzed and he quickly picked up, but once again, Arlene beat him to it. "Sir you have a message from Thomas Begay wanting to know if you could meet him at the *Dinébikeyah* Cafe for lunch before noon today. He's at the payphone down at the Co-op."

Charlie glanced through the outer office to see Arlene meet his gaze a questioning look. "Dial him back, Arlene, and tell him, I'll be there." The last thing Charlie wanted was to field a time-consuming interrogation from Thomas Begay. There still was a stack of morning reports he likely wouldn't finish this afternoon. But he was only five minutes from the restaurant. The more he thought about it, the more he felt he should have pursued his talk with Billy Moon a little longer, yet her mental state had appeared so fragile he had been reluctant to press her any further. He might have to rearrange his thinking in that regard... and soon.

5

The Crucible

Pulling into the *Diné Bikeyah*, the first thing Charlie noticed was the string of Tribal police units around the front door. *Well, either the place has just been robbed... or the chicken fried steak is back on special... That always draws a crowd.* Arlene generally called the cafe early in the day to check out what the special was, and then posted it on the office bulletin board. Several of the staff counted on the posting—for a few it was the highlight of their day.

Sure enough, the "cop shop" table was full-up. And the table next to it was, too. He spotted Thomas Begay sitting alone at a small table in the middle of the room. There had been a time when the man had been on a first-name basis with most of those officers—a tenuous relationship at best.

Thomas smiled grimly as he indicated the full table with his chin and shrugged. "I was lucky to save a seat for you. They're having one of their 'schools' according to my nephew. I spoke to him coming in and was told he'd already had this 'school' once. I guess he was determined to stick it out for the free lunch."

Charlie glanced over at the booth and Billy Red Clay waved at them. The young officer picked up his cup and headed their way.

As he approached the table Thomas glanced up at him. "Well, Nephew, how goes the school this second time around?"

Billy put his cup down and, grinning at his uncle, took the remaining chair. "Tribal's paying for lunch today. You wouldn't want me to pass that up, would you?"

Charlie nudged Thomas, glanced over at the coffee station, rolled his eyes, and whispered, "That's why he decided to take the class over. Your nephew has a lady friend." The investigator directed his interest elsewhere, as the waitress, pot of coffee in hand, headed their way. Then in a less audible tone, "I'm guessing the cop-shop wasn't in her section today?"

Billy frowned, which quickly changed to a grin as Irene came to a stop and waited for the two older men to turn up their cups. Billy pushed his cup toward her, and the girl began filling it as she touched him on the shoulder, as though to steady herself. "Hi, Billy," She frowned as she poured for the other two. "I'll be back with some menus in just a sec."

Charlie held up a hand and indicated Thomas with a toss of his head. "I don't think we'll need menus; we'll both have the special." Indicating Thomas with a toss of his head. "And Billy here already put his order in over at the 'cop' table." Putting away her pad and pencil, the young woman quickly made her way back to the kitchen as Charlie and Thomas exchanged grins.

Billy shot a look at his uncle. "That's the new girl, Irene. The old Irene moved to Gallup."

Thomas stared after the young woman, then turning to his nephew, nodded, "I know who she is…or was before she got married." Picking up his cup he blew on it before taking a cautious sip. Raising an eyebrow, he glanced at Charlie. The two had been friends since boarding school and were each attuned to the other's thinking. Charlie glanced the girl's way again, but saw her differently now, not in a bad way, just not the same.

"Oh, I didn't know she was married." Billy was clearly taken aback.

Thomas could see now how things were and sighed as he put down his cup. "She isn't married now, as far as I know, but she was a while back. I didn't know she'd moved back up here."

"Moved back, from where?" Billy was attempting to sound casually indifferent but missed the mark.

Thomas thought a moment, "She's been down in Grants from what I heard...couple of years now."

Billy gazed down into his coffee then giving the two the side-eyes, said, "Well, I just came over to say hi... I better be getting back to the guys. I think those are our food orders coming." The liaison officer walked back to his table, not quite as chipper as he'd come.

Charlie considered Thomas for a moment before saying, "The boy wasn't expecting that. I think he's pretty high on the girl. You might want to take it easy with him until we see how Irene really feels."

"If I'd known, I might have kept some of that stuff to myself, maybe." Thomas sighed audibly, "Billy's a grown man. This is just more man-stuff—he'll be fine."

Charlie frowned. "This isn't what you called me down here to talk about, is it?"

"Not really...but closer than you might think."

"What's that supposed to mean."

"I came down here to tell you my wife thinks she knows something you might want to hear. Lucy had a council meeting today, so she's made me the messenger. Did Billy ever mention Irene's last name?"

Charlie thought about it a moment. "I'm not positive but I seem to remember him saying it was Nez."

"That was her married name."

"And…?"

"Her maiden name was Kly." Thomas waited for this to sink in.

"As in *Rupert* Kly?"

"One and the same. Old Man Paul T'Sosi, once gave a sing over at the Kly camp and Lucy Tallwoman went along to help. It was so long ago she hadn't remembered until she met Billy Moon at your birthday dinner. She's positive Billy Moon is the one they gave the sing for. She thinks the girl was a teenager at the time, and very pregnant."

"So, how is this Irene Nez related to Rupert Kly?"

Thomas glanced around the room and lowered his voice. "That's where it gets a little sticky. Paul T'Sosi said Rupert was the girl's 'uncle,' he thought" Thomas hesitated a moment, glancing toward the coffee bar, before going on. "Paul mentioned later he thought Rupert might have been the father. How he knew this, Paul never said, but Lucy thought one of the Kly women had once hinted he should give the girl something to get rid of the baby. You have to understand, these were rough people who mostly stayed off to themselves in the back country. In those times it would have been very danger-ous to get involved in such affairs. Paul knew that. You know as well as I do, the old man was not the kind to do anything of the sort they were asking about."

Charlie glanced up as Irene brought their lunch and realized now why she seemed familiar. How he could have missed it he couldn't imagine. She was nearly a ringer for Billy Moon when the woman was young—her grey eyes being the clincher.

With a twinkle in her eye, the girl put down the platters, saying, "I had them send extra gravy on the side. That's how Billy likes his."

When Irene left the table, Charlie found he had lost some of the appetite he came in with yet did his best to make a good show of it. Thomas, on the other hand never let anything get in the way of eating.

After finishing lunch, Charlie didn't wait for the check, he knew what the price of the special was, doubled it, and added enough for the tax and a hefty tip besides. It was his turn. As they were leaving the cafe, they raised a hand at Billy Red Clay, which he acknowledged with a somber lift of his chin.

Outside, the two men stopped beside Thomas's old diesel truck. Charlie being the first to speak. "Lucy didn't happen to know what became of the Kly family did she?" He paused to think back… "Or, even if Rupert Kly was still alive?" Billy Red Clay's mom said she didn't know…and hadn't heard anything of them in years."

"No, Lucy didn't know anything beyond what I told you. People on the *Dinétah* moved around a lot more back then. I expect they could be most any-where…if any are still alive." Thomas grew quiet and Charlie knew he was thinking about what had been said here today and this caused him to wonder what may not have been said, as well.

Charlie was reluctant to say anything further but felt it had to be said. "I don't think we should mention any of this to Billy, not right now anyhow."

Thomas nodded thoughtfully, and replied, "I think you could be right."

Charlie tried to lighten up the mood. "What are you doing this afternoon?" Something had occurred to the investigator, and it wouldn't wait.

"Oh, not that much, what did you have in mind?"

"I was thinking of taking a ride out to the fair-grounds and maybe having another little chat with Billy Moon. I thought you might want to tag along if you ha-ven't anything better to do."

Thomas nodded. The man's tone led him to be-lieve he might want some company, or maybe even a witness. Not that Charlie would ever come right out and say so. "That sounds like it might be fun. Sure, I'm up for that." He had known Charlie for many, many years. Longer even, than he'd known Harley Ponyboy. There was very little Thomas wouldn't do for either of the two men.

~~~~~~~

They could see from a distance there wasn't much going on at the fairgrounds. A few stock show participants who'd stayed in town to shop for groceries or buy feed at the Co-op. Some lived a good distance away and for them, this would be a last chance to stock up before winter was on them. Once the weather changed these people might not be able to get to town as much as they liked.

Charlie pulled up just inside the gate and turned off the engine. Only one lone food truck was left near the main tent, and it appeared to be open, possibly reluctant to leave off what had been a lively and lucrative weekend for their business. "How about a cup of coffee, Thomas? You're not too full for that, are you?"

The pair got out of Charlie's Tribal unit and stood there a moment, as they eyed the fairgrounds. Charlie spotted Billy Moon's motorcoach back behind the stage area, which was already being dismantled and loaded on trucks. The two men wandered over to the concessioner's truck as they took in the tearing down and packing up of what had obviously been a well-attended event. The owner proved to be a Navajo woman and her daughter from Chinle, Arizona. The woman smiled and Charlie ordered two cups of coffee. "You're in luck," she said, "I was about to throw it out. I made more than we needed…it's still fresh though…and it's on the house."

The men nodded their thanks. The woman set a bowl of creamer on the counter and a box of sugar packets to go with it. When she brought the steaming cups, Thomas asked, "How was business this year, good I hope?"

"Not too bad. I wish they'd advertised that Billy Moon was on the program—I honestly think they'd had twice the turn-out."

Charlie glanced over at Thomas, and then turned to the woman. "Oh, I'm sure that's right… Isn't that her tour bus over there behind the stage?"

"Yes, it is. I've talked to her several times. She seems very nice for someone as famous as she is. I didn't know she was going to be here at all but when my daughter heard about it, she just had to go see her show…and me along with her. We had to shut down the truck for two hours, but it was worth it. We could have heard it all from right here, of course, but there's nothing like being right up front when she's preforming. Did you ever see her?"

Charlie grinned, "Not this time I didn't, but I saw her a long time ago. She's something all right."

"Yes, she is. Me and my girl can't believe we were lucky enough to be here at the right time." The woman cleared off the coffee fixings and put them in a box under the counter. "She sends her driver over now and then to get something to eat for the two of them, but she don't come out much, except to perform."

"Aw, that's too bad, we were hoping we might get to see her around the grounds today." Thomas was just making conversation, but he sounded sincere enough.

"Well, probably not, I guess. She left out of here early this morning in her new vehicle and hasn't been back as far as I've seen this afternoon, but then I've been busy packing up and might have missed her." She turned to her daughter. "Have you seen her come back, Mary?" The teenager hadn't said a word since they walked up, and now just shook her head and turned back inside.

Charlie nodded and thanked her again for the coffee as Thomas left a tip in the jar she had sitting on the counter. The two Navajo meandered off as though they were just killing time.

When out of earshot, Thomas said. "Looks like we missed her."

"Looks like it, I guess. But I'd like to take a look at that bus as long as we're out here. I've never seen one of those things up close."

"Are you thinking about buying one?"

"Well, not today, but who knows what tomorrow might bring." Charlie was in a good mood, and it was contagious. Both men were laughing by the time they ambled up to the bus.

Thomas stood, hands on hips, looking it over. "I'll bet that that thing is nearly new. What do you suppose one of those would cost?"

"I read somewhere it could be as much as a million dollars or more depending on the options and all. I don't know that for a fact. But I think that's what I remember the article saying."

"Wow, I'd sure like to see what it's like inside."

A rough voice from behind had them both whipping around. "That's not likely, friend, we don't give tours." Facing the man, both were surprised at the size of him.

"*We*? Is that your bus, 'friend'?" Thomas said this in a pleasant enough manner and was smiling, too, but Charlie knew that could change in an instant.

The big man didn't bother to say anything, just started around them. Charlie reached out and grabbed Thomas by the arm just as he moved to tap the big man on the shoulder. Charlie had been down this road a few times and figured this might be their last chance to opt out of something really ugly.

The man, evidently hearing the shuffle of feet behind him, whirled around so fast both Navajo stepped back in surprise. "I hope I made myself clear," he said, but deeper in his throat this time.

Charlie cursed under his breath and put his hands up, one of which held his badge. Thomas glanced at him without saying anything, hoping he wasn't putting too much faith in this show of authority. Ever the lawman, Charlie shook his head at his friend in such a way Thomas knew he meant business and stood down.

The big man probably weighed over two-sixty and at six-five, there wasn't an ounce of fat on him. His ears were cauliflowered worse than any Charlie had ever seen. Most of his front teeth were perfect—too perfect to be his. A rough purple scar ran from his left ear to the lower edge of his jaw. Clearly, he was a man who at some point, might have made his living beating people up. His arms hung loose at the side and the knuckles on his ham-like fists appeared to have been broken many times by the mass of scar tissue over partially fused bone. The man's expression had not a hint of animosity—calm and unworried, like a man going to work. He peered at Charlie's badge. "Cop?"

Charlie was inclined to say yes but didn't think it well advised. "I'm Investigator Yazzie with Legal Services." He reached in his pocket, and saw the man tense, as he retrieved a card and held it out to him. "We're friends of Billy Moon's. Maybe she mentioned us, she was at my office this morning."

The man took the card, though he had trouble holding it in the battered hand. "We don't talk much, me and Billy," he said as he studied the card. "Everyone who comes around says they're a friend of hers. But the truth is, she has few friends that I'm aware of." He looked up, "She's not here right now, but I'll tell her you dropped by when she gets back." Then, with hardly a glance, he turned on one foot and was gone.

Thomas let out a deep breath, as Charlie stood with a stunned look on his face. It was the first time he'd ever seen Thomas Begay rethink a fight.

The lanky Navajo shook his head. "I don't know what the hell I was thinking. I doubt both of us together could've made a dent in that guy." He chuckled with a faraway look in his eye. "I'm glad Harley Ponyboy wasn't here with us... We'd all three be in the hospital by now…or worse. You know how Harley is…he just don't think things through, like I do."

Charlie gave him a look from the corner of his eye but didn't bother saying what he was thinking.

On the way back into town neither of the two said much. Thomas did admit, however, they might want to take more help if they were to go back out there. He gazed out the window as they came into town and mused. "That old boy seemed calm enough, easygoing and all." He let out a deep sigh. "But, he's the kind that will break a person's neck without even thinking about it." He turned to Charlie, "I've only ever seen one or two like him. But, like a rattlesnake—even if you've never seen one—you know in your gut, you should just leave it be."

Nodding, Charlie glanced over at him and said softly, "I guess we just got lucky this time."

6

The Murder

Driving home that afternoon, the smell of late Autumn swirled in on the breeze. The cottonwoods along the river had already lost most of their leaves and were looking a little embarrassed. The cool damp air wafting in off the muddy banks of the San Juan had a nip to it he recognized. It was the tail-end of his favorite time of year. It wouldn't last long, and he knew he should be making the most of it.

The investigator was having a little trouble putting the events of the day together. *If what the old singer, Paul T'Sosi thought happened back those many years ago at the Kly camp—was in fact, what had happened.* He was beginning to consider another reason Billy Moon might have returned to the reservation. He played this around in his mind the rest of the way home.

The cement-colored sedan in his front yard sported government plates, only adding to the sense of foreboding he'd felt since lunch. Agent Smith was not in the habit of making personal calls. Fred must have checked with Arlene, only to find he was already on his way home, then decided to meet him half-way which in itself, was a cautionary indicator.

Pulling into the yard alongside the sedan he spotted the FBI man sitting on the steps of his front porch. A hint of relief appeared on the agent's face as Charlie hopped out of the truck.

"There's no one here, so I decided to make myself at home." He stood and extended a hand.

Charlie shook hands. "What's up, Fred?"

"Rosemary Kly is dead, Charlie. I'm on my way out there now. Forensics is already en route."

It took the investigator a moment to recall whose name this was. "Rupert Kly's wife? Who reported it?"

"Her daughter, Gladys Nez—Nez is her married name. Rosemary had been staying with her and her husband, Lester for the last few weeks. Gladys being pregnant, I guess she thought she needed her mother to be there. Apparently, the baby's due any time."

"Cause of death?" Charlie knew it was too early for the question but hoped to at least get some sense of what happened. The woman had to be along in years, an accident maybe.

Fred was noncommittal. "Not sure until I get out there and talk to forensics. Since your office has been working with Billy Moon and inquiring about her family, I thought I'd ask if you wanted to ride along on this one… And to be honest, I'm not too sure how to get there?"

Charlie rubbed his forehead, trying to think. "Sure, Fred, let me leave Sue a note and I'll be right with you. Uh…what sort of directions did they give you?"

"They said take 491 south and then the Sheep Springs turn off into the Chuskas. They said they would have someone out there to lead us to their camp. I'm thinking it's going to be rough getting in there."

"We better take my truck, Fred. It *is* rough country and not much of a road once you're off the highway. We can drop your car off at Legal Services to save time on the way back. I may be stopping by my office on the way home anyway. Arlene could have left a message or two."

Fred scratched his chin as if considering this, then shrugged. "Let's do it then."

Charlie hustled into the house, used the restroom, and left a note for Sue on the kitchen table. He was back in less than ten minutes, to find the FBI agent already in his car and ready to go.

"How far do you figure it is, time wise?" Fred asked as he rolled down his window.

"Hard to say. Depending on the state of the road it could be as much as two or three hours, hopefully less."

Fred nodded. "Maybe I should have stopped for some water and something to eat, should we get caught out. I never even thought of it. I've been stuck in the office too long, I guess. I know better, just not thinking." The agent shook his head and looked away. "Just getting old, I expect."

Charlie was aware Fred had grown up in this part of the country and was a little surprised to hear him say he hadn't thought of these things. He laid it off to the man's slow recovery from the old head wound but had not noticed any lingering debilities before. *He's probably just tired,* the investigator finally decided. "Fred, I have some stuff behind the seat I carry for just such emergencies. I think we'll be all right. Hopefully, we'll be home before it becomes a problem... Let's hope so anyway."

They made good time as long as they were on the highway, but as Charlie had feared, once they ran out of pavement, things changed for the worse. The road was graveled for the first quarter mile or so, but that quickly turned to dirt, and then only a rutted two-track, more of a trail than any kind of road. As it got rougher, Fred had to brace himself against the door, and Charlie even caught himself holding onto the dash from time to time.

Fred believed the forensics people had started out a good bit before he did. "I would think they should be somewhere ahead of us by now."

"Depends on what kind of vehicle they're driving, I suppose. Whose meeting us out there from Tribal?" Considering who the man's liaison officer was, Charlie guessed it would be Billy Red Clay. The FBI man quickly confirmed that was indeed who it would be. Nothing could have pleased Charlie more. He liked Billy and was happy to see him involved as Liaison. The young officer was finally going somewhere at Tribal, and no one deserved it more. He was well liked, and no one worked harder at his job.

The two men jolted along in silence for another mile or so before the Agent spoke again, almost reluctantly, or so it seemed. "We have turned up a little more information you might be interested in." He frowned, "I haven't had time to write it up, but here's the gist of it. Billy Moon has as much money as most people think she has, and possibly a great deal more. Her finances are muddled, as you might expect from someone who makes a living on the concert circuit—a lot of those gate receipts are cash. My people tell me there's no real way to know for sure. From what we've learned she has very good accountants and bookkeepers, but a lot of her assets are liquid and privately held." He paused for a moment before smiling as he said, "I understand you've met her driver Tito Alverez, the woman's long-time driver and bodyguard. One time prizefighter, he later became a guest of the government for a few years. He was in for murder, bumped up from manslaughter by virtue of his being a professional fighter. Someone sprung him early. Someone with a lot of money and good lawyers."

Charlie wondered how Fred knew about him and Thomas being out there…and so soon, too. It had only been six or seven hours. *The FBI has their ways all right*. Over the years he'd found it best just to assume the Bureau knew all and saw all. He was careful now to figure this into every single equation when dealing with the agency.

"So, what's their relationship, Billy Moon and Tito, I mean?"

Fred chuckled, "It's a hard one to figure. He's been her bodyguard since her early days on the concert circuit, but that was about the extent of it from what is known. I suppose the man feels he owes her. He's unquestionably loyal from what we know. What was your impression, Charlie?"

81

"Just about that, I guess. He claims the two of them seldom talk on a social level, but I will attest to his loyalty. Not much gets past him." Charlie was now even more curious. To his way of thinking, Tito Alverez didn't add up. "No further problems with the law after his release?"

Fred sighed, "Clean as a whistle. There have been rumors, but nothing you can hang your hat on. Either complainants have been paid off, or there aren't any left to complain. The scary thing about that is, we know there have been incidents, but no one ever comes forward, not even a casual witness…simple as that."

Charlie swerved to miss a jackrabbit, only to run over a clump of sagebrush, instead. Regaining control, he smiled his apology. "I know I shouldn't swerve for that kind of thing—and I know a lot of people have been in wrecks doing it, too." He thought a moment. "With me it's just second nature to give them a miss when I can." The investigator shrugged, "I'm really not sure why either. Growing up, I shot many a rabbit for the pot, but killing one for no reason just doesn't seem right. Old time Navajo thinking, I guess. Harley Ponyboy says his family would have starved if not for eating rabbits."

Fred Smith nodded as though he understood…and he probably did.

Charlie peered through the windshield. "Is that someone up ahead?" Daylight had been slipping away to meet a new moon, and the ensuing dusk was making it difficult to see.

Fred leaned forward in the way a person often would when he wanted to make out something at a distance…even knowing five or six inches wouldn't make a difference. "It's a man…and it looks like he's flagging us down."

As they drew closer, Charlie spotted the Tribal patrol unit backed into the sage. "That's Billy Red Clay all right."

Though he was going less than fifteen miles an hour, which he was convinced was his limit, he nonetheless started braking. The person in the road turned on a flashlight and stood to one side. Pulling even with him Charlie rolled down the window and held up a hand. "I guess this is the place?"

Billy came closer and shook his head. "Not exactly. It's on up that little canyon to your right. It's a pretty good climb. You'll have to watch that edge too. I don't know why…in the hell, people have to live in places like this. I've already been up there once and there's not much room to get around 'till you get almost to the top."

"Get in, Billy, no need in beating both these vehicles to death. Did forensics get here?"

Billy climbed in the back seat before answering. "They're not coming. They radioed to say they took the wrong turn-off and, on top of that, their truck broke down. I expect it will be morning before they can get a tow-truck out there."

Charlie half turned, surprised, "We didn't hear anything on our radio"

"Well, you might have shaken something loose coming in. Ain't that a hell of a road?" Billy nodded to the FBI man, "How are you, Fred?"

Fred Smith was still frowning at the radio but raised a finger in greeting. "Damn," he said under his breath. "I heard some static back up the way but couldn't tell who it was or what they were saying." Fred reached out and tried turning it off and on a time or two. "It looks to me like it's completely dead now."

Continuing down the road, many a rueful stare was directed at the errant radio, dark and silent. Occasionally, Charlie would reach over and give it a couple of hard whacks with the heel of his hand…Still nothing. Finally abandoning the effort, he glanced back at Billy in the rearview mirror. "So, what is the story on the deceased? Where was the body found? Could you get any idea what happened to her?"

The young cop thought briefly before answering. Looking from one to the other of the two men, he cleared his throat as he hooked a thumb back over his shoulder, saying, "Well, we're already past the place where the body was found. That was down at the highway. Rosemary's daughter says the woman had told them she was going to walk down to the trading post, or maybe catch a ride into town if they didn't have what she wanted. She apparently thought there were some things they needed before the baby came. They said she'd already decided it wouldn't be coming as soon as they first thought. Apparently, the men were all off gathering stock, and Rosemary didn't drive. She hoped to catch a ride back with a neighbor who had gone to town earlier that day. Gladys said her mother had sometimes done that in the past."

Charlie interrupted, "I didn't see any neighbors."

"No, not down here, but there are a couple of families on up above here, hard as that might be to believe. About another mile up past the daughter's camp, the country opens up a good bit. There's a couple of catchment basins that hold enough stock water to last through the summer…most years. She said there's a lot of good sheep pasture up there, even enough for a few cows early on."

"So, who brought the remains back up here to their place? The people who live in this area wouldn't seem like the kind that would stop and mess with a corpse, no matter who it was." Charlie was pretty sure of this.

"No, they're not. The body was off to the side of the road... Some people on their way home spotted it, slowed down enough to see who it was, and then came on up to tell the family. Her daughter, and her husband, when he got home, brought the body back up here by themselves... Afterwards he drove back out to the trading post to notify the authorities, then came back up again to be with his wife." Billy Red Clay took a deep breath and said, "I'm the one who took the call when it came into the office. I got ahold of Fred, and you know the rest."

Fred murmured to himself, "I wish they hadn't moved the body. Forensics isn't going to be happy about that...if they ever get here."

"I asked the couple up there why they decided to go down to get the woman," Billy replied. "They said the coyotes was bad this year and they weren't sure how soon anyone would make it out here—they didn't want to leave her out there by herself overnight."

"Someone could have stayed down there with her till morning, couldn't they."

"They didn't want to do that either. The daughter is due to deliver any time now and thought it would be bad for her to be around such a business. And it wouldn't have been right for the son-in-law to stay down there with her—you know how that works. They have the body up there in the summer hogan on a cot covered up with a tarp. They said they would tie the dog up out there tonight and it would let them know if anything comes around... The husband said it's a big dog."

Charlie spoke up. "You all know they're going to want the body out of there as quick as they can." Looking at Fred Smith, he added, "They won't wait long."

The FBI Agent nodded matter-of-factly, "I know that. We aren't here to tell them otherwise, either." The FBI man probably knew as much about *Diné* customs as any white man and was fully aware they would have to make this quick. "Our obligation at this point is to determine a cursory cause of death and verify the woman's identity." Fred pointed out across the face of the bluff. "There's plenty of people buried out here with less than that. The Bureau learned long ago that interfering with traditional burial rites can wind up being a lot more trouble than it's worth." He paused and looked at the two Navajo law men. "That is...if foul play is not indicated. If that's the case, it's our job to see that the remains are taken into Farmington for autopsy and the medical examiner's determination."

87

The *hogan* was situated on a bench just below the rim. Most of the camp was taken up by sheep corrals and a lambing shed, leaving little room for parking more than a couple of vehicles. Charlie couldn't figure why they would put a camp here and said so.

Billy Red Clay was able to answer that question. "The husband said there's a good spring here and shelter from the wind and snow. He says it's a good place to lamb their ewes. They take them up on top to summer them. All these people up here are related to each other one way or another. It's a tight clan and they've been here a long time. Gladys's husband is not from around here. He met Gladys Kly at boarding school. He says she's not at all like most of her family. They only moved back up here so she could be near her mother."

"So, Rosemary's husband Rupert Kly lives up there on top, too?" Fred Smith obviously had a reason for asking.

Charlie wondered if it had anything to do with Billy Moon's father, and if the FBI man might have decided to reopen the case. He meant to ask him when they had a moment alone. Fred could be a stickler when it came to privileged information.

The Tribal policeman glanced up the road. "I understand Rupert and Rosemary and their daughter, all moved up here from Crown Point, back when my own people lived there. That's been a long time ago, I was just a little kid myself when we moved to Shiprock."

The FBI agent took out a small notebook. "What are the people's names that live here?"

Billy took out his own, identical, notebook and read. "The daughter's name is Gladys. Her husband is Lester. Last name is Nez."

Fred asked Billy Red Clay to go up and keep the daughter and her husband busy, while he and Charlie took a quick look at the remains of Rosemary Kly.

The summer *hogan* was more substantial than most, with a good lay-up of stout posts on the west side to block the sun. A large white dog came out to the end of his chain and stood silently taking their measure.

"That *is* a big dog." Charlie acknowledged. "An Anatolian with a little something else in him, if I'm not mistaken. There's getting to be a lot of them here on the Reservation…used for guarding sheep mostly. The coyotes are bad everywhere since the cut-back in government trapping."

Fred came up, and the dog immediately took a more aggressive posture and began barking. Charlie walked up closer to the animal and started speaking Navajo in a low voice. He turned to Fred. "I think he's all right if we move along that side wall and just take it slow and easy." He smiled, "I doubt he's ever seen a white man in a suit before." And then. "Looks like he's on a pretty short chain … Shouldn't be a problem."

Fred moved a little closer to make his own assessment of the dog—and the chain. Following Charlie over to the far side of the brush shelter, they eased up next to the cot at the back of the enclosure. The dog followed their progress for a moment, then turned a circle and laid down facing them, not taking his eyes off the pair.

"Catch the other end of that tarp, Charlie, if you will, and we'll fold this to the side a little, so we can see better. Are you going to be okay with this, Charlie?" Fred knew from working with the Tribal investigator over the years that the dead did not intimidate him as it did some. But still, it was only polite to ask.

"I'm fine, Fred." Charlie really wasn't fine, but he was up to the task.

The woman's head pointed toward the investigator and Fred was at her feet—one of which he instantly noted was twisted at an odd angle. Charlie studied the face of the dead woman…serene and without the slightest mark or abrasion which surprised him somewhat.

A soft voice speaking in Navajo came from the front of the shelter. "Her left hip is broken, and her ankle is shattered. That's what my wife said when we moved her last night." The two looked up to see Rosemary's son-in-law standing beside Billy Red Clay and the dog.

"We heard the barking and figured I'd better come down and see if everything was all right. He's a good dog, you know and never bit nobody yet, but with strangers you never know what a dog like this will do."

By strangers, Charlie knew he meant Fred Smith, which was likely the first white person this dog had ever seen.

Charlie, falling into Navajo himself, answered the man, "How is your wife doing, Lester? Okay, I hope? I mean, what with the baby coming and now this... We can take her into town if you like and have the clinic check her." Charlie glanced at Fred and could see by the look on his face they would have to wait for Forensics. Switching tact's he said, "I'm sorry, Lester, I'm afraid we will have to leave your mother-in-law here until the forensics team can get here. They will have to transport her to Farmington to be examined by the coroner. It appears she's been hit by a vehicle. And accident or not... We'll have no choice now but to try to find out what happened." Charlie's Navajo had been a little rusty when he first came back from university but was much better now. He thought the man might be more comfortable thinking the white man didn't understand what they were saying. Fred, for his part, knew very well what Charlie was doing and went along with it. This sort of news would be easier for the man coming from a *Diné,* and in his own tongue.

Lester nodded slowly and, glancing at Fred a time or two, turned back toward the main *hogan*, probably to tell his wife what must be done about her mother.

Billy Red Clay waited outside the summer *hogan* while the men covered the body. Charlie knew the young officer was not comfortable around the dead and would avoid it whenever he could. But like himself, Billy did not let it interfere with his work.

When the two men came out of the arbor, Billy said Gladys Nez told him that when her father heard the police were there, he got in his truck and left by the back road. There were a lot of gas field roads in that area, and if a person knew his way around, it wouldn't be hard to keep out of sight, especially this close to dark. "Gladys didn't appear so happy about this. I got the feeling she and her father don't get along."

"Did you ask what sort of vehicle the man drove?" Charlie didn't intend going after him in the dark, but he did intend to find the man, one way or the other.

"It was an old red Chevy, a flatbed with most of the paint worn off. She didn't know what year." Billy shook his head. "It's a shame what that woman had to go through last night, going down there to get her mom and all. Now, Gladys thinks the baby's going to come soon…tonight maybe. She thinks it might be affected by what's happened. Her husband is on his way up to the other camps to see if one of her cousins will come down to be with her. She has an aunt up there too, but she's old now and doesn't see very well. Her cousins have both had kids themselves and know what to do should something not be right."

Charlie nodded, thinking, *most Diné women who have herded sheep and been around ewes at lambing time, have the basics imprinted on their minds from childhood.* He looked at Fred as he said, "Our women are endowed with genes gained over thousands of years of selective evolution to handle the birthing process with as few problems as possible." He grinned sheepishly, as he realized what he'd just said. "Of course, that's easy enough for me to say. I took my wife to the hospital for both our two kids."

Billy shook his head, "Well, Gladys seems pretty sure that baby is coming tonight. I told them if they needed to contact someone on the radio, I would be happy to do it. I think those two are good people…but I'm not too sure about the rest of them up there." The young cop smiled. "Lester and I parted company on pretty good terms."

"Who do they think ran over Rosemary Kly last night?"

"Oh, you know, Charlie… they wouldn't say anything about that, even if they did know. That's just the way they are out here. I'll keep talking to them. Maybe someone will let something slip…but I wouldn't expect much help from these people."

"Billy, you okay with staying on here until Forensics can make it up. I doubt it will be before noon tomorrow. But they might fool us and get here earlier."

"Sure Charlie, I know someone has to stay and you and Fred will have to be back in the office in the morning. This is part of my job. I don't mind doing it. I'll sleep down there in my truck tonight." He grinned. "It won't be the first time."

Charlie Yazzie was a person who took his own job seriously and appreciated the trait in others. He knew not everyone felt that way and he admired Billy Red Clay for it.

7

Crosstrack

On the way back down the bluff they dropped Billy Red Clay off at his truck to make sure the forensics team didn't get lost again. Another vehicle might have to be sent out for them along with the tow truck. Billy, of course, would have to take them back up to the *hogan* to pick up the body. He doubted their ambulance/van would make it up there, even though it was four-wheel drive.

"I hated to leave Billy up there by himself." It wasn't hard to see Fred's concern for the young officer was genuine.

"He'll be fine. I left him the emergency supplies I carry and the water. I'd be surprised if those people didn't invite him to eat with them, too."

Fred laughed. "Well, I suspect he wouldn't have had it any other way. I've never seen an officer his age with such diligence when it comes to his work…or one my age either, for that matter."

Charlie chuckled and then said, "Fred, let's see if we can figure out where Rosemary was run over. I know it's dark, but the place should be right up ahead here somewhere, according to what her son-in-law told Billy." He slowed the truck and the two men rolled down their windows and put their heads out as Charlie turned on the spotlight.

"What about up there by that little juniper tree? Looks like the shoulder gravel's torn up some. Like someone may have tried to turn around or maybe swerved or something."

It was on Fred's side of the road, and as they got closer, he held up a hand to stop. "Looks like someone may have got out, here, all right."

Charlie eased the truck forward but stayed on the pavement. He reached down and flipped the switch on the blue and red light bar and put on his flashers as well. There was virtually no traffic this time of night, still this was the way he was supposed to do it, and he tried to follow the rules as much as possible.

Fred reached for Charlie's flashlight and studied the ground. "Whoever it was wore cowboy boots…about like everyone else in this part of the county. Must have been an awfully small guy from the size of the prints. As you saw up at the Nez place, Rosemary was wearing sneakers."

Overall, there was little to be seen that either of the two lawmen thought important enough to get out and risk destroying what little sign there might be. They knew Billy would look things over after daylight. He wouldn't have much else to do until forensics got there. The young cop was known to be good at securing a crime scene. He wouldn't miss much if it was there.

~~~~~~

Charlie let Fred off at his car in the Legal Services parking lot. He doubted the man would get much sleep before it was time to head for the office. He was still a little worried about the agent's state of mind. He knew the man was worn out, but there was something else there, too, and it bothered him. Fred Smith was the best senior agent ever appointed to this regional office. Everyone had missed him when he was out on medical leave, and Charlie thought it would be a shame to see him suffer some sort of remission when he had been coming along so well.

~~~~~~

Harley Ponyboy was up feeding his mules as the investigator left for work the following morning, and came over to the driveway, waiting for the Tribal unit to pull even with him. "How'd it go up there? Sue said you might be out all night." He leaned in closer. "Something about someone found dead up in the Chuskas, she thought."

"Yes, an older woman, maybe a hit and run. It was a little after the Sheep Springs turn off. Billy Red Clay is up there now waiting on a forensics team to show up."

"You don't know who did it?"

"Not yet we don't, but we'll all be working on it today. Maybe Billy will have something more for us when he gets in."

Harley shook his head. "Well, that's too bad. Who was the woman anyway?" Harley could see the Investigator was in a hurry, but he was curious and wanted to know.

"Her name was Rosemary Kly. I'll tell you all about it tonight when I get home."

Harley nodded and backed off as Charlie gunned the engine and headed for town.

~~~~~~

Charlie checked in at the office, picked up his messages, and told Arlene he was heading over to the motor pool to have his radio checked out, and then out to the fairgrounds to talk to Billy Moon about a few things. "I should be back by lunch, and if not, I'll let you know."

The woman watched him as he left the building. "He's not going to be back by lunch," she murmured to herself. Arlene had evolved a sixth sense when it came to Investigator Yazzie. Which is probably one reason they got along so well.

The two-way radio's problem had been correctly diagnosed by nearly everyone the night before. It took only twenty minutes to trace the blown fuse to a loose wire that had rubbed itself into a short. The mechanic who fixed it suggested Charlie should have examined it a little further the night before. It would have been an easy fix, he said.

At the fairgrounds, Charlie, seeing the place was now nearly abandoned, pulled the Tribal unit across the empty space where the stage had been and parked not twenty feet from the big man washing the tour bus windshield. Turning off his engine he got down from the truck, resting an arm on the front fender as he watched the man work.

As Tito Alvarez turned and looked at the investigator, it was without the slightest hint of recognition. He quickly turned back to the window he was working on; obviously worried about the soapy water drying on the glass before he could get it rinsed off. It was a big windshield, and he wouldn't want to do it over again.

Billy Moon stepped out just as Charlie started toward the door of the coach. Waving, she said, "You look a little tired this morning, Investigator, how about a cup of coffee?"

Charlie smiled and nodded. "Looks like you're about the last one left out here, Billy."

"Yep, Tito said the food truck pulled out yesterday while I was gone. It's just the maintenance men and us left now, I think." She climbed back into the bus, leaving the door open for him to follow.

Charlie glanced over at Tito and knew he'd been watching him in the windshield's reflection. He touched a finger to the brim of his hat. But the man didn't turn or give any sign he'd seen the gesture. Wiping the dust off his boots on the doormat, the investigator climbed into the interior. He paused at the top to take in the spacious salon. He was frankly amazed at the degree of opulence lavished on this coach and could see now why they cost what they did. Elegantly sculptured carpet ran the length of the bus, set off by luxurious wood trim.

The sumptuously upholstered dining area, fitted in burgundy leather, was done with black marble countertops and stainless appliances framed in elegant mahogany. Charlie imagined this was what a fine yacht must look like inside.

Billy Moon waved him over to the dining table, saying, "Have a seat, Charlie, make yourself at home. Coffee will be ready in a minute." The woman seemed at ease in a white T-shirt promoting a Paris music festival paired with jeans neatly tucked inside western boots. He couldn't help noting how small her feet were.

Etta James crooned softly in the background. He didn't know what he had expected, but it wouldn't have been Etta James. Billy poured coffee and brought it to the table on a tray with cream and sugar.

Charlie said, "I didn't see your car when I pulled up...I was afraid for a moment I might have missed you."

"Oh, that thing I leased wasn't what I thought it would be at all, it wasn't built for this kind of country. I turned it in this morning. My fault probably, I'd forgotten how rough the roads were out here. The dealer's bringing something else out this afternoon...hopefully, something I can get around in a little better."

"Ah...Out sightseeing, then?" Charlie made a mental note to have a chat with the Ford dealer.

"I guess you could say that. I haven't been back in so long, I just wanted to look around a little."

The investigator took a sip of his coffee, admiring the ceiling, a long oval mirror enveloped in the headliner, with hidden lighting glowing softly around the periphery. "This certainly is an impressive coach, Billy. I had no idea they were so luxurious."

"Well, when it's the only home you've got, it's nice to have something you can live with, I guess, and, then too, it's what the fans expect. It's just the way things are done in this business."

Charlie looked away as he unconsciously toyed with his spoon. "I'm afraid I may have some bad news for you, Billy. It's about your Aunt Rosemary."

There was a sharp intake of breath as the woman straightened in her chair. The smile faded as though a shadow had fallen. Her eyes remained fixed on him as the breath left her. "I haven't heard that name in a very long time." Her head canted to one side. "What happened to Rosemary?"

Charlie wanted to be perfectly honest. "It looks like it may have been a hit and run...possibly an accident. We're waiting for a report from forensics and the medical examiner. We left one of our own people out there—Billy Red Clay. You may remember him from the party. I expect we'll hear more this afternoon.

Autopsy reports won't be in until tomorrow late most likely." Charlie watched closely as the woman digested all this, if she was feigning shock, she was making a good job of it.

"Where is her husband, Rupert Kly?"

Charlie cleared his throat. "We don't know...He was out there earlier, apparently, but disappeared by the time we arrived. We have an all-points out on him. From what the FBI says, he is not thought to be a sophisticated person and there's a good chance he'll be apprehended soon."

"And his other sister, how is she?"

"There is only one of them up there. She's still in the camp with two of your cousins and their husbands. Rosemary had a daughter who was about to deliver a baby...That has probably already happened."

"What is the daughter's name, do you know?"

Charlie thought a moment.... "Gladys. She's married to a Lester Nez. He's not from this part of the reservation...they met at Government Boarding School, I believe. I have no idea which one."

"There should be another girl...a little younger than Gladys. Do you know anything about her?"

"We were told Rosemary had two daughters...one was said to have died some years back. I don't have her name. The FBI is working on all these details. They won't release them until they are verified and, I'm not sure how long that might take." While Billy Moon was processing this, Charlie happened to look up through the windshield, and in the right rearview mirror, he could see Tito Alvarez sitting quite still on the lower step, seemingly listening to their conversation.

Billy Moon sat pale and drawn, her breath shallow. Showing little emotion, she stared at Charlie as though something had just occurred to her. "And what of my father...is there anything new concerning his death?"

"Of that, I can only say my conversations with Federal Agent Smith has left me hopeful there will be an investigation within the Bureau. I'm near certain Fred will reopen the case. Much of the evidence he's gathering is slanted toward your father's death. The death of Rosemary Kly has temporarily taken his attention, but in the end, even that might prove important in the investigation of Wayne Moon's death." Secretly noting Billy's expression, Charlie again saw little sign of what she might be thinking.

The woman glanced up at the clock, and he thought this might be a hint he should be going. He quickly put down his cup and mentioned an appointment in town, saying he would be back in touch when he heard from the coroner's office. The investigator stood up to leave, only to find Tito Alvarez standing behind him. The man was like a cat and had come up on him without the slightest sign.

Tito avoided eye contact, staring past him as he spoke. "Billy, the dealership is here with another car. They'll need to have you sign some paperwork."

Tito moved out of the investigator's way without a word, and Charlie slipped past him and down the entryway steps without glancing back. At his pickup, the investigator took note of the new rental parked off to the side—a tan-colored four-wheel drive Jeep, a hardtop with dealer plates. Two men from the dealership stood near another vehicle chatting in the sun. The Fairgrounds were quiet now and abandoned but for a dust devil twisting its way across the parking lot. It would soon be winter, though possibly a mild one from some reports. He frowned to himself. *No one really knows ahead of time what the weather will be on the reservation. That was the one thing you could be sure of out here.*

~~~~~~

On his way back to the office and coming up on the Diné Bikeyah cafe, he noticed Thomas Begay's truck in the parking lot and whipped in thinking he might as well see what was going on with him, and maybe have an early lunch while they caught up. Thomas would want to hear about the goings on up on the Chuskas.

The investigator had beaten the lunch crowd and quickly spotted the tall Navajo at a table in back. Thomas started talking to him even before he reached the table.

"What the hey, Hastiin? I called your house last evening, and Sue said you were down-country looking into a death in the Chuskas. What was all that about?"

Charlie sat down, motioning to a waitress as he turned his cup over. He went into the happenings of the previous afternoon and night. A waitress he'd never seen before was there with the pot within a moment or two and filled his cup as she nodded to him. She held up a finger to Thomas and said before he could complain, "They're running a little late in the kitchen this morning—had a leak in the fryer, I guess. I'll be right back for your order." She smiled engagingly. "I'll put a rush on it."

Thomas waved it off as she left, and then took a sip of coffee. "So, Rupert Kly slipped out the back door on you boys up there, ehh?"

"Yes, he did, never saw hide nor hair of the man... Fred and I had been hoping he might be up there, and he was just too slick for us."

Thomas grinned. "I would have thought my nephew would know to circle around and secure the perimeter."

Charlie frowned as he fixed his coffee. "Well, he didn't know the man was up there, for one thing, and we were a little busy at the time."

"You should have called me. I could have shown you both how it's done."

"I'm sure you could have, but Fred came by the house and was in a big hurry to get up there." He shrugged. "Fred's a busy man these days, I guess. He's short-handed and doing a lot of the filling-in himself." Looking around the restaurant, the investigator asked, "Who's the new waitress? And where's your nephew's girlfriend?"

Thomas shrugged. "Her name is Millie, and she's filling in for Irene...who, apparently, didn't show up for work this morning."

Charlie thought about this before posing another question, but Millie was on her way over, order pad in hand. He thought it best to hold off until she was out of earshot.

When the woman had left the table, Charlie remembered what he was about to say before the interruption. "You mean, Irene didn't even call in sick or at least have some kind of excuse for not coming in?"

"No, she didn't, and that's another reason they fell behind this morning. Millie claims this was supposed to be her day off at her job over at the Co-op. But she finally agreed to come in, you know, because she has experience in the restaurant business. She didn't want to burn any bridges, she said. Still, it was plain she didn't like being called in on such short notice."

Charlie looked toward the kitchen. "I've never seen *that* woman over at the Co-op, either...In fact I don't think I've ever seen her, period."

"She hasn't been here long...moved in from over around Tonalea. She works upstairs in the office. From what Robert over at the Co-op says, she should have stuck to waitressing. She's having a hell of a time with billing and such. That's just according to him, of course."

Charlie could always count on Thomas for the latest in local news. How he managed to find these things he didn't know, but he did.

"I believe Billy Red Clay will be back this afternoon sometime, and I'll bet he will be a little put out that his girlfriend isn't here."

Thomas nodded. "All I can say is, Irene better have a damn good excuse for not coming in this morning. That old lady who runs this place will fire her in a heartbeat. She doesn't put up with any such nonsense as that. I've seen it before."

Charlie just shrugged, seeing their cheeseburgers and fries were on the way. *Good thing they got that fryer fixed* he thought, as Millie set their platters down. *A cheeseburger with no French fries would not have gone over very well in this establishment.*

Thomas looked up, locking his eyes on something. "Oh, oh, here comes the man."

Charlie glanced up from squirting catsup, as Billy Red Clay trudged through the door, all dusty and gritty looking. The Tribal policeman pulled his hat off and hit it on his leg a couple of times, knocking the dust off, then slapped at his pants with the hat a few times before searching for them. He'd obviously spotted their vehicles in the lot. Or else the young cop was there on other business...*Monkey business, more than likely,* Charlie thought. *That young man is going to be disappointed when he finds no Irene to serve him.*

Thomas chuckled. "Looks like he could have knocked that dust off outside, wouldn't you think?"

Charlie nodded. "Probably a good thing Irene isn't here to see that." Both men smiled to see the cashier glaring at Billy Red Clay, police officer or not.

Billy was almost to the table when he paused with a frown on his face. Stepping up, he glanced back at the coffee station. "Where's Irene? She's supposed to be on today."

Neither man said anything. Thomas reached across for the catsup bottle as though he hadn't heard. Both went on eating as Millie, spotting the newcomer, headed their way with the coffee pot and a smile. The woman obviously did have some experience in the business and knew how to handle herself when the chips were down.

"How did it go up in the Chuskas?" Charlie brushed some dust off the table where Billy had rested his elbow.

The policeman held up a finger. "Let me get this order in—I'm starving." He stared at the waitress a moment. She certainly wasn't Irene. "I'll have same as these two, but make it a double…with extra fries."

As Millie left the table, writing as she went, Thomas started in on him. "So, you let that big bozo get away from you up there in the mountains, huh, Nephew?"

Billy frowned. "I didn't let him get away. We never had him to start with…didn't even know he was up there." *Charlie must have already told him everything.* Billy knew his uncle was just having a little fun with him but wasn't in the mood for it, and it showed.

Charlie hadn't abandoned him, however, and stepped up to share the heat. "Billy did a good job up there. Of course, we all know you could have done better."

"Yep, I could have." Thomas stuffed several fries in his mouth, then talking around them he said, "You two should have taken me and Harley along with you."

Both men ignored this, and the investigator again asked Billy what had happened after he and Fred left the Kly camp.

"Not a whole hell of a lot, Charlie. The forensics boys got up there early, and I hauled them up to the camp to retrieve the remains. And, the baby had come during the night, so the medical guys agreed to check it over before they left. Lester and me, we talked some this morning before I started down the canyon. He seems like a real decent sort, and so does his wife. He said Rupert and Rosemary hadn't gotten along with each other in years. They didn't even live together anymore, according to him. Rupert stayed in the upper camp, and Rosemary spent most of her time down below with him

111

and Gladys. He spent most of his time over at his second wife's place. Apparently, Rosemary had seen the poster for Billy's show down at the trading post and told her husband she was going into town to see her." Billy gave the pair a knowing look. "Rupert said she'd better not do that if she knew what was good for her. They had quite a row over it from what Lester said."

Thomas narrowed his eyes and said in a low voice, "Sounds like he didn't want her talking to Billy Moon. Maybe afraid she'd tell her something, or vice-versa."

Billy Red Clay nodded. "I think he's afraid Billy Moon has come back for a reason, and that the reason might be him."

Thomas peered across the table at Charlie. "That makes sense to me. Why else would Billy Moon come back to the reservation—there's nothing else here for her."

"Maybe, but we don't know what's in the woman's mind, do we? We'd best try to figure that one out *before* we go off half-cocked." Charlie didn't like the way things were shaping up and thought it time to do something about it. "I've got some people to see today, and this isn't getting it done." Standing, the investigator said, "I'll see you boys later."

Thomas wrapped what was left of his food in a napkin. "Mind if I tag along? I'll worry about you if I don't." The man said this with a grin, but it was plain he was determined to go along.

Charlie didn't have time to argue the point, so only sighed and nodded. *It might come in handy, having a witness along who speaks good Navajo. It might help eliminate a lot of problems on down the line.* They left Thomas's truck at the cafe and, with Charlie at the wheel, headed toward the Four Corners Monument.

8

The Suspect

Charlie pointed the Chevy pickup northwest on 64 to Teek Nos Pas, then hooked a left on 160 toward the Four Corners cutoff, only a couple of miles past the junction. He glanced over at the lanky Navajo sprawled against the passenger-side door, dozing comfortably in the weakened rays of a midday sun. A high band of cirrus had drifted in from the west and was doing its best to make a little shade. *Well, I guess Thomas is right. He doesn't look at all worried now that he's along for the ride... Not that he's aware of it.*

It had not taken the investigator long to discover the whereabouts of retired Tribal policeman Robert Hoskinny. Several of the older officers at Tribal remembered him quite well—one even knew where he currently lived. It turned out the old man had a trailer house in an isolated area of the reservation, just west of the

Four Corner's marker. A flat desolate area with little in the way of redeeming features. *A hell of a place to finish out one's life,* the investigator thought.

Charlie waited until turning off the highway before nudging Thomas awake. "It's only another five or six miles according to my directions," he said. "An old blue trailer with a few corrals and sheep pens. Should be on your side of the road."

Thomas stretched and rubbed his eyes briefly as he gazed around the Godforsaken countryside. "Seems like someone who'd been with Tribal police all those years could have done better than this."

Charlie frowned. "At one point I guess he did do better—had a nice little cinderblock government house in town. But gave it to his daughter and her kids. They were trying to live out here, and not having much luck at it. He moved in here by himself after his wife died. He told a friend the place suited him—he had grown up out here and never liked living in town anyway, he said."

"Well, I've heard that tune before. There's not many left who are able to make any sort of life in this kind of country. No TV or phones…have to haul your water…and it's a long way from a store, too. So, he did have a wife, huh? How long has she been gone?"

"I didn't ask."

Thomas nodded. "By hell, I might already know the man. I've done business with a lot of cops in my earlier days." He chuckled under his breath. "Due to the circumstances, I may not recall their names, but I seldom forget a face."

"This looks like the place coming up, on that little knoll." Charlie pulled into the sandy track up to the trailer as several big dogs appeared as though out of nowhere. In the yard, the two men stayed in the truck as Charlie beeped the horn a couple of times.

The door opened a crack and, after a moment, the man appeared pulling on an old, frazzled Levi's jacket. Recognizing the Tribal emblem on the truck, Robert Hoskinny raised a hand in greeting. But didn't come off the small wooden porch.

Charlie rolled down the window and, smiling at the old man, said. "Those dogs going to be alright with us getting down?"

"Oh, they'll be fine, just don't try to pet 'em...they'll be fine. You with Tribal police?"

"No, we're not. I'm with Legal Services in Shiprock."

"Who is that you got there with you. Is he with Legal Services, too?"

Charlie stepped down from the truck, eyeing the dogs as he came toward the porch. "I'm Investigator

Charlie Yazzie." Thomas wasn't far behind, as Charlie aimed a thumb over his shoulder, and said, "This is Thomas Begay here with me, his wife is on the Tribal council, you may have heard of her, Lucy Tallwoman." Charlie threw this in on the off chance it might lend some slight redemptive factor to Thomas, should the old policeman recognize him. Thomas and Harley Ponyboy had cut a wide swath through this country in the old days. He and the old man might well have run into one another in his line of duty.

The ex-tribal cop peered at Thomas a moment without saying anything but did finally invite the two in. "Come along then. I'll scare up some coffee."

The old man set a pot of coffee to perk, and as the two settled themselves at the table, he leaned against the counter as if studying his guests at close range. Staring at Thomas Begay he asked with a wry smile, "Where is your little friend Harley Ponyboy? What's he up to these days? You two are staying out of trouble now, I hope."

Thomas chuckled. "Yes, we've pretty much outgrown those youthful ways."

The old man nodded, a hint of doubt hanging behind his eyes. Turning to the investigator, Robert asked, "So, what is it I can do for you boys today?"

Charlie scratched his head. *This old man might be a little sharper than he figured,* causing him to become even more hopeful the visit might yet lead to something. Pulling out several folded papers from his jacket pocket, he said, "Mr. Hoskinny, these papers are from an old case file, a report you turned in some years back." He set the copies on the table and tapped them with a fore-finger. "If you could just take a look at these and see if there's anything you might now remember that was not in the report? I know it's been a long time but thought you might now recall some small something you didn't think to write down back then—maybe something you didn't feel was important at the time."

The retired policeman passed them cups and spoons, and then moved on around the table where he sat and putting on a pair of old spectacles, began reading the papers. Halfway through he motioned Charlie to reach for the pot and fill their cups, which he did keep-ing one eye on Robert for the slightest sign of something he was at odds with or surprised at.

Thomas didn't see any milk or sugar but didn't say anything, knowing nowadays, many older people were suffering from diabetes in one form or another and pur-posely didn't keep sugar in the house… Others, of course, just couldn't afford it.

Finally putting the papers down, Robert took a cautious sip from his cup and declared, "I remember the incident…and the people involved. It may sound strange, but it really doesn't seem that long ago to me. These things were a part of my life and what I did for a living. This wasn't my first run-in with Rupert Kly. Tribal had sent me out several times before on domestic abuse calls. Rupert was a big rough man and liked to knock people around when he was drinking, and he was drinking a lot at the time. Those charges never came to much, however."

"Why is that, Mr. Hoskinny? Those are serious accusations. It would seem to me someone would have preferred charges against him."

"Well, you would think that. But you have to understand those were different times. One of the man's brothers was on the Council, and a clan uncle was prominent in one of the Tribal legal agencies. Those people wouldn't want to risk that kind of publicity."

Charlie looked up from his cup and asked. "What about murder, Robert, would they risk that?"

The old man adjusted his eyeglasses and peered down at the papers for a moment. "What murder, Investigator?"

Thomas and Charlie glanced at one another. "The murder in that autopsy report, Robert...Wayne Moon's murder."

The old policeman appeared to consider this for a moment. "That autopsy report says cause of death:

119

Undetermined. It would seem to me there *was* no murder, according to the medical examiner."

Charlie smiled and nodded. "Didn't you think that was a little strange, Mr. Hoskinny? The medical examiner didn't say death due to exposure, or natural causes, or anything else. Just, undetermined. Didn't you think that was a little odd, Robert?"

"I have never seen this autopsy report before today...until just now. The medical examiner, at the time resigned shortly after and was dead of what was said to be cancer within six months."

"Do you recall the coroner even coming out to the death scene?"

"No, I don't, Charlie. My partner and I were the responding officers from Tribal. We waited until the body was picked up for autopsy, but I don't recall the Medical Examiner being with them."

"Would your partner be able to verify that?"

Robert sighed deeply. "I'm sure he would. If he were alive. He died several years ago at home, of a heart attack. He was retired like me."

Charlie sat back in his chair and placed his hands on the table. "Robert, the FBI is more than likely going to reopen this case, and when they do, they may call on you again. If there is anything you might recall later, I would appreciate it if you would give us a call." Saying this, he retrieved a card from his wallet and handed it to the retired Tribal policeman."

Robert Hoskinny studied the card a moment and then said. "I guess there is one last thing you might want to know. Rosemary Kly followed me out to the truck that day and told me in private, that Rupert had been abusing their adopted daughter, Billy. She said the man had threatened to kill her if she told anyone. I could see she believed him, too. You might want to talk to her instead of me."

Charlie looked up at the ceiling and sighed. "So, you haven't heard then? Rosemary Kly was found dead up in the Chuskas a day or so ago, a hit and run... An accident maybe?"

A shadow crossed the old man's face. Shaking his head, he whispered, "I knew Rosemary from the time we were kids growing up. That's the only reason she told me. I sent those reports through, but like always, nothing ever came of them—I doubt very much Rosemary's death was an accident."

Charlie rose to go, and Thomas stood as well. The investigator then hesitated, as though he too had remembered something. "Robert, do you recall what agency it was that Rupert's clan cousin worked for?"

The old man looked him straight in the eye. "It was Legal Services, Investigator."

On the way back into town, Thomas Begay didn't say much, just focused his attention on the scenery, or lack of it, gazing out the side window like a man undecided. Finally, he looked over at Charlie, and wondered out loud. "Who was the 'cousin' at Legal Services, do you suppose?"

"I've been thinking about that myself. It may have been close to the time I started there, probably about the time of the big power shift in Tribal government, the one involving nearly everyone on the Council at the time, including the chairman. That regime had been in control of things for several years and left a shadow on Legal Services which lingered for some time after they were gone." Charlie concentrated on the road ahead but felt the color rising to his face as he went on. "Fortunately, most of those people are now either in prison or no longer alive." He turned a grim face his way. "They got what they deserved, that's for sure."

"You should have asked that old cop who it was…at Legal Services, I mean."

"I think I already know who it was."

Thomas waited for him to say a name, and when he didn't, became quiet for a space of several miles. But, when he could stand it no longer, blurted out, "Well, who was it then…for God sakes."

"He's dead now, Thomas, it doesn't really matter who it was. When I get back and have a little free time, I'll check into it a bit further. It's not important now…but I'll check into it. It would be interesting to know for sure, just for the hell of it, I guess. Should I find out anything for certain, I'll let you know."

Thomas nodded and sighed—having already conjured up several suspicious characters in his own mind.

Charlie asked, "Do you think you might have time to stop by the Ford dealer in Farmington with me? I'd like to have a look at that black SUV Billy Moon turned in the other day."

"Yep, time is the one thing I've got plenty of. I need to pick up my truck at the cafe anyhow, so no big deal."

~~~~~~~

Under a lowering sky, Charlie pulled into the dealership in late afternoon. Rain possibly turning to light snow was the forecast on KENN. Looking northwest he conceded the weatherman might be right for a change.

The two men stood a moment in the show room admiring the new cars, and though neither favored this brand of vehicles, there was just something about any new car that excited their interest. A salesman had seen them pull up in the Tribal unit and must have doubted they were serious buyers. Consequently, the man took his time coming over.

"How are you gentlemen today? Anything I can show you this afternoon?"

Charlie drew his jacket back to expose the badge clipped to his belt. He said politely enough, "Yes there is, we'd like to speak to the manager, if it's not too much trouble?" He passed the salesman a card. "You can say it's a matter of official business, if you like." The man nodded suspiciously, giving Thomas a once over, thinking he might be a disgruntled customer come to file a complaint. It wouldn't be the first time.

The manager, when he came from his office, had a scowl on his face. But as Charlie stared him down, flashing his badge, the man seemed to rethink his first impression of the two. "Come on back gentlemen." The man was probably thinking it better to sort this out in private rather than the showroom, which still had a few customers meandering about.

As they followed him back, Thomas whispered, "Why is it these car salesmen are the only people who ever call me a gentleman?"

Charlie laughed. "Maybe he just made a mistake," then grinned at the expression on his friend's face.

Sitting across from the manager, the pair watched silently as he cleared a few papers from his desk. Looking up, he murmured, "Sorry about your wait, gentleman. What can I do for you this afternoon?"

Thomas was thinking *what? No introduction or handshake? This is why Dapper Dan's car lot gets all the reservation trade. These people here have no manners.*

Charlie, ignoring this lack of common courtesy, got right to the point, holding up his badge as he said. "A Ms. Billy Moon recently rented or leased a new SUV from you folks and then later returned it for something different. Do you recall that transaction?"

The man didn't have to think about it. "Yes, I do. I handle all the rental paperwork myself. I believe the car is still in the detail shop, but it's ready to go back on the lot if you would like to see it."

"Oh, what sort of work was done on it?"

"No work really, just the standard detail wash and vacuum we do when sending one back on the line. We can walk out the back way here and have a look. May I ask why you are interested in the car."

"Certainly. We are friends of Billy's, and Thomas Begay here was so taken with the car he thought he might be interested in buying it when she turned it in. He's a great fan of Ms. Moon and since he's looking for something for his wife, he thought it might be nice to have this vehicle. Mrs. Begay is on the Council now. She needs something a little more upscale, if you know what I mean?"

The man rose instantly then, "Ah, I see. Well then, if you gentlemen would just follow me…My name's Eddy Baker, by the way. The vehicle has barely been used at all…can't tell it from a new one, actually."

Thomas remained stone-faced during the entirety of the conversation as though he might not speak much English. Like most *Diné,* Charlie knew there was nothing Thomas liked better than taking part in a good joke, especially on someone like this haughty car dealer.

Sure enough, the unit was sitting just outside the shop doors, still dripping a little water from the undercarriage. The two Navajo slowly circled the Ford. Thomas making various unintelligible noises, possibly expressing his opinion of the vehicle. Charlie turned and spoke to him in Navajo, basically just warning him not to overplay his part.

Thomas answered in Navajo, to say something like, "Don't worry about a thing... I've got this."

The manager trailed behind, obviously anxious to learn what the man might be thinking about the vehicle. Charlie could picture the salesman mentally calculating how far he might push the price. Charlie was paying particular attention to the front-end of the big Ford, checking for recent bodywork or new suspension parts. Thomas, taking his cue from this, got down on all fours, and rolled partway under the car and checked out the suspension. Then, coming out with a frown he rattled off several points that needed addressing, all in his native tongue, of course.

Charlie turned to the dealer. "My friend says they missed a few spots underneath. And he wonders if there has been any bodywork on this front-end...says the paint looks a little funny to him."

The manager got down on one knee and tried to peer under the vehicle without getting his dress pants wet at the knee. He really couldn't see much, good, or bad. "There's never been even a scratch put on this car, as far as I know. We look them over very carefully when they come off lease... There's few small rock chips in the front-end paint, maybe, but that's hardly avoidable in this part of the country." He appeared to be wondering what he might say that could help. "Hmm... I'll have the boys re-do the underside for you, it's a little late in the day now, but I can have it ready first thing in the morning if you'd care to drop back by for a second look—bring Mrs. Begay along and take it for a drive. I'd be happy to arrange it for you."

The dealer walked around the vehicle, opening all four doors to show off the sumptuous leather upholstery. His face lit up as he said excitedly, "This interior is in absolutely mint condition, as you can see. Top of the line…actually. And take a look at that odometer. The car has less than 500 miles on it, and I put 100 miles of that on it myself. I occasionally like to take one of these nicer one's home for the evening, just to keep myself familiar with the line." He smiled hugely at the two. My wife loved it too, by the way. I'm sure Mrs. Begay would enjoy driving this car for years to come. Not a nicer one in San Juan County."

Thomas was still frowning and muttering to himself as he shook his head at the car. Then in a louder tone began to express his opinion on everything from the color to the condition of the carpets. It was obvious to the dealer the man wasn't pleased for some reason and was, in fact, fast losing interest.

Charlie listened carefully and translated what he wanted the dealer to think had been said. "Well, Eddy, it seems it's his wife's birthday next week and he doesn't want to present her with a car that's lacking in any way. He says he will think it over and call you if they're still interested." Shaking his head he mumbled, "Sorry, Eddy."

Thomas turned with a grim face to lead the way back through the dealership and out to Charlie Yazzie's Tribal pickup.

The dealer stood, still holding the front door open and waved a weak goodbye, a disappointed little pout pulling at the corners of his mouth.

Charlie, opening his door with a sad look on his face, waved the man good day. Starting his truck, it was almost impossible to keep a straight face long enough to make it off the lot. Then no longer able hold it in, the pair broke into gales of laughter. "That wasn't very nice of us, now, was it?"

Thomas shook his head. "No. I feel bad for carrying on like that…but it was fun, huh?"

Both men laughed again for a mile or so when Charlie grew serious. "I don't think anyone has been run over by that SUV lately, do you?"

"Doesn't look like it, does it?" Thomas sounded somewhat wistful when he added, "I wish I was able to buy that car for Lucy, she really would have loved it. Did the man ever say what the price was?"

Charlie thought about the question as he drove and frowned as they blew through the township of Kirtland. "You know, I don't believe either of us thought to ask the price."

Thomas looked over as Charlie's face grew more serious. Having a good idea what his friend was thinking, he asked the logical question. "So, you think this rules out Billy Moon as the driver who ran down Rosemary Kly?"

"Well, it pretty much looks that way to me…right now at least. I mean except for those small boot-prints Fred saw at what we *thought* was the scene of the accident. Which you'll have to admit is thin evidence." Charlie was beginning to feel a little dispirited by his initial suspicions not adding up as he thought they would. He sighed. *This must be how it feels to be forty years old.*

"When did you say that autopsy report on Rosemary would be in?"

The investigator thought a minute. "Two or three more days at least. That's what Fred is thinking now. And that may be only a preliminary report. If he decides to send something to Albuquerque for further analysis… Well, that could complicate things."

Thomas shook his head as he gazed off into the distance. "Sounds to me like everything is going to be up in the air until you're able to go over that autopsy report. And what bothers me is; what if Billy Moon decides to leave the country. Once she takes off in that bus of hers, she could wind up being damned hard to track down. You noticed her coach didn't have any kind of graphics alluding to whose rig it was. Not a single promotional image on it. She could be a little harder to find than the average celebrity—if you know what I'm saying. Harley and I both have thought from the start there's something a bit wrong about the woman."

Charlie shot a glance his way but remained silent. He was having a harder time reconciling his view of Billy Moon as a murderess. After talking to her the last few days, he was certain she had the motive, but was now less convinced she had it in her, to outright kill a person. Especially not a helpless woman. Rupert Kly, on the other hand, was a different story.

He had expected Agent Smith to have a lead on the man by now. Still and all, he, himself, hadn't turned up anything new, either. Thomas, Harley, and Billy Red Clay had been scouring the country for some word of Rosemary's husband, but they too, had come up empty. There was no doubt something would turn up; it was just a matter of time, as they say. *The only question being who will get to him first?*

9

The Mystery

When Agent Smith called the next morning, Charlie could tell by his voice he had come across something important. Fred seldom showed any great excitement, no matter what the situation. This time it was clear the man was agitated. The fact they had missed their opportunity to apprehend the prime suspect at the Kly camp, and by only a few minutes, must have stuck in his craw.

He barely waited for Charlie to say hello before declaring. "One of my people may have a fix on Rupert Kly. My agent was down at the county jail questioning a suspect in a gun theft case when Rupert Kly's name came up. Our guy recognized it from the bulletin we put out after our little trip to the Chuskas. It seems the thief had sold the handgun to Rupert only a few days ago. He claimed it wasn't the first time he'd sold stolen goods to the man—he'd known him for years, he said. The seller let it slip that Rupert has another wife over near Round Rock in Arizona. Not all that far from the Kly camp in the Chuskas—not as the crow flies, anyway. The Agent told him he would put in a good word for him in the theft case if he would tell us who the woman was and where she lived. The person said the woman lives in an old traditional *hogan,* and that Rupert hangs out there sometimes, adding, "It's a hard place to find if you don't know the area."

Charlie hesitated a moment before asking, "Fred, have you sent anyone out there as yet?"

"No, I haven't, and much as I would like to go myself, I'm the only one in the office for the next two days. We have a new agent coming in from Albuquerque, but in the meantime, we are short a man. In any case, after giving it some thought, I was wondering if it might not be best if you and Billy Red Clay tried to slip up on him out there, assuming he's there. You will need to talk to someone who can pinpoint where the place is From the information I have, it can be hard to find. And, it is said, they can see someone coming from a long way off."

"What about going in at night?"

"I thought about that, but from what we were told it's hard enough to get to in daylight."

Charlie was already nodding silently. "What do you think about me taking Harley and Thomas along? Those two can come in handy at times. They know that country and understand how to talk to people out there. Then too, we might have need of a good tracker… should things go south."

Fred didn't answer for a moment but when he did, he made his official position clear. "Charlie, you know I can't authorize the use of civilians in an operation like this. But privately, I wouldn't object to you engaging them under the auspices of Legal Services." Charlie knew Fred was aware it would be a good deal easier for an all-Navajo team to work this maneuver. "How soon do you suppose you could you put this together, Charlie?"

"As soon as I can round the guys up, the sooner the better. We'll try to get there well before dark and then figure out what we are up against before deciding how to make our move. We can't use my official unit, too easy to spot. I'll ask Billy Red Clay if we can borrow one of the vehicles they've confiscated. He said last week they have two or three in the impound lot over at Tribal. If not, I'll talk to Harley Ponyboy about his truck. I wouldn't want to try sneaking up on anyone in Thomas's diesel rig. I'll take my unit in as far as the trading post and use whatever else we find to go on in from there. At least that way we'll have a radio available nearby if something happens that requires a call for backup."

Fred said he thought this was better than anything he had come up with so far and gave Charlie his rather sketchy directions to the woman's camp, whose name, he said, was Glynda Benally. Then wishing them luck, said, "Don't hesitate to call if you need us. I'm sure Billy will alert Tribal police should things get out of hand." Fred left off with a warning, "I know I don't have to tell you this man is dangerous and probably armed. Don't take any unnecessary chances. We will catch up with this guy eventually no matter what, but it would be nice to put a lid on it now."

~~~~~~~

Within two hours the four Navajo were loaded up and on their way, down 160 out of Shiprock, then 191 to Rock Point, where for the sake of maintaining some degree of anonymity, would leave Charlie's truck at the Trading post, continuing to the cut-off to the Walker Creek crossing. From there on it would get tricky. They would eventually be nearly due east of the Kly Camp on the other side of the Chuskas…but a long way around by road, if it could be called that.

Billy Red Clay had felt none of the confiscated vehicles from the impound lot would be reliable enough for such an undertaking. They didn't have to ask Harley Ponyboy twice—the man was quick enough to volunteer his own truck, too. He declared he would rather be in his newer Chevy as it was already outfitted for off-road travel and well maintained.

Pulling into the trading post where they were to drop off Charlie Yazzie's Tribal unit, the investigator and Officer Red Clay rolled into the far end of the parking lot and parked facing the paved road. The lawmen stayed in the Tribal unit, while Thomas and Harley Ponyboy drove his Chevy right up in front of the store where they could be seen getting out. The man and his wife who ran the place would know everyone in the area and be on a first-name basis with most. One of them would know exactly where Glynda Benally lived and the best way to get there.

Charlie figured Harley and Thomas would take their time finding out what was needed in the way of directions. The old couple would be cautious and a little suspicious of these strangers. He also knew the pair would load up on whatever snacks they thought necessary for such an adventure, short though it might prove to be. Should it be decided to wait and move in under cover of darkness, however, those snacks might come in handy.

It was more than thirty minutes before the pair came out of the store, followed by the trader, himself, who continued to speak as he came, pointing toward the distant bluffs making up the western side of the Chuska Mountains. "Once you get to the creek crossing, you'll see a road of sorts veering off to the south toward the bluffs. When you come to a big dry wash, you'll see vehicle tracks going back up the wash to the bluffs. It's not really a road you understand. It's just a way a'goin I guess. You'll climb out of the wash in a little break in a bend in the wall. Once you top out, you'll be able to see the Benally *hogan* in a little cut in the bluffs to your right. It's hard to spot, so you'll have to look close to see it."

Charlie could hear all this from the open window of his truck as the old man, being hard of hearing, was also a 'loud talker'. He could see in his rearview mirror the outline of the man's wife standing in the open doorway, gazing toward their truck. *Not that concerning,* he thought. *Tribal patrol units would often stop in such a place for the officer to eat his lunch or even take a little nap should things be slow.*

The four men waited until the Trader and his wife headed back inside the store. Only then did Harley Ponyboy start his engine and run the truck up toward the road. Looking back at the store, he pulled up to Charlie's unit and the two lawmen climbed into the Chevy with Harley and Thomas.

Charlie, in the backseat with Billy Red Clay, tapped Thomas on the shoulder, "Well, that looked like it went pretty well."

Thomas chuckled and glanced back at him. "It took a while. These old traders are careful of their customer's privacy when it comes to strangers. Harley here, was able to convince the man he was a clan member of Glynda's and was bringing her some things from a relative in town."

Charlie leaned forward. "Did anyone happen to mention Rupert Kly's name?"

"Not really. Harley managed to work the conversation around to Glynda's 'husband' and ask if he was home or not. The trader and his wife just sort of looked at each other until finally he said, the man seldom came by this way and didn't know if he was out there or not. Later, the wife did mention they hadn't had much traffic for the last day or so. Only a lost tourist in a fancy new jeep had stopped for a cold drink and a little general information."

Charlie perked up at this, thinking. *That's inter-esting.*

Billy Red Clay nodded. "I can understand that; there's not a whole helluva lot in the way of road signs out here, as far as I can see."

Thomas went over the directions to the Benally camp. "From our conversation, I'm certain, if Rupert Kly is out there at the woman's place, he didn't come in this way. More than likely, he came across on the same four-wheel drive road he used to escape you boys up at their camp the other day. If he's here, he's been here a while, I'll bet. He'll be watching this way in for sure."

Billy Red Clay snorted as he scowled at his uncle. "I'm telling you one last time, Uncle Thomas, the man didn't *escape* from us. We didn't even know he was up there at that upper camp until his daughter's husband told us that he took off when he heard we were down below at their place."

Harley chuckled from the front seat. "He's a sly old fox, all right. We'll have to watch him, or he'll get away from you boys again."

Billy passed a hand across his face while shaking his head, obviously aggravated. Thomas opened the bag of snacks, candy bars mostly—except for a package of miniature chocolate covered-doughnuts. Everyone knew they were Thomas's favorite, and he opened the package with the obligatory gesture of offering them around.

Charlie threw an accusatory glance his way. "All you bought were candy bars and doughnuts?"

"It wasn't a health food store, Charlie. I'd bet these doughnuts were about the healthiest thing in the place." So saying, the man popped one in his mouth and began to chew contentedly.

Charlie glanced out the side window thinking, *this reservation must be a major distribution point for chocolate-coated doughnuts. It's hard to find a place, that doesn't carry them.*

Heading northeast on the cutoff put them on a stretch of dirt road that had seen very little maintenance over the summer. Everyone grabbed a handhold as Harley fought the wheel, barely able to keep the truck in the ruts. Slowing the Chevy to a crawl made travel easier but still bone rattling.

Billy Red Clay hadn't said much since they took the cutoff, but now offered his take on their chances of apprehending the wary and elusive Rupert Kly. "There's some big country behind that *hogan,* but not many roads from what I see here on Tribal's map of the area. If Rupert gets loose back in there, he's going to be hard to dig out. I was thinking we could stop just before we top out of that dry wash the trader was talking about. They can't see us down in the wash and it would be a good place to leave the truck." Scanning the skies for clouds and not seeing any, Billy offered up a few thoughts on the weather as well. "I don't think there's much chance of a rain this afternoon. So, it should be all right to leave Harley's truck down here in the wash without it getting carried off by a flashflood of some kind. "

Harley scanned the sky suspiciously knowing it could rain twenty miles away and still send a flood through there.

Billy Red Clay went on as though he hadn't noticed. "I'm wondering what the chances are of someone slipping up on top for a little covert look at the lay of the land?"

Charlie nodded. "Could be a little risky, but maybe worth it if we can figure out something that would allow us to wait until almost dark, then split up to cover as many escape routes as possible, there can't be more than one or two I would imagine." "

Thomas Begay glanced at the men behind him, eyebrows raised. He couldn't think of anything better, but still felt uneasy with the idea and said so. "Who-all brought a gun…anyone?"

Charlie held up a finger, as did Officer Red Clay, of course. Harley then said, "Mine's in the glove box."

141

Thomas smiled "Well, that makes it unanimous I guess."

Charlie again held up a hand and declared. "Whoa, there shouldn't be any call for anyone other than Billy and me to be armed going in up there. We represent the law...so to speak."

Harley looked in the rearview mirror and smiled. "Whatever you say, Investigator. Whatever you say." The two men in the front seat exchanged glances and grinned.

The rutted two track had turned to little more than a jarring trail of buried rocks and deltas of small arroyos issuing from the massive wall of sandstone bluffs just to the east. Billy said he thought they should be getting close to the gap that would take them up on top.

Harley suddenly dropped the speed to a crawl and, with a push of his chin up the wash, said, "Looks like someone beat us to it."

Charlie quickly leaned in to see around Harley. Spotting a vehicle pulled close into the lee of the wall, he noticed the driver had nudged the front end of the Jeep right up to a good-sized boulder. Focusing as best he could, the investigator said, "I hope that's not who I think it is."

Thomas peered through the dusty windshield. "Are you saying that's the Jeep, you told me Billy Moon switched to when she turned in her other rental?"

Closer now, Charlie said, "It looks like it from here." He reached inside his jacket and loosened the .38 in his shoulder holster. "How in the hell did Billy Moon find out where Rupert was before we did?"

Harley seemed to be concentrating on the tire tracks in front of him. "Looks like that Jeep came in a good while ago. The wind just started blowing around noon. And already the tire tracks are drifting in. I'd say it's been parked here since mid-morning. Just a guess of course, until I can get out and have a closer look."

"Ease up beside it, Harley...about as close as you can get." Charlie was fairly certain it was the same vehicle the Ford Dealer delivered out to Billy's coach at the fairgrounds. He could see the dealer plates from here but that was about all he could see. "I can't see anyone in it."

Billy Red Clay, having the youngest eyes in the bunch, said, "There's no one in it unless they're hiding...or dead. Pull up beside it, Harley, so they can't open the doors on this side. We'll have it boxed right up against that boulder in front. Then we can pile out here on the offside with plenty of cover from your truck."

Harley frowned but did as the man suggested, assuming the officer had training in this sort of thing.

Billy squinted an eye at the jeep. "When you come even with it, shut your engine off and keep your head down. We'll cover you from outside."

Charlie nodded guessing Billy must have learned this in his last school. It did sound like it might be the safest way to go about it.

Before Harley shut the engine down, he shot a quick glance into the other vehicle. "I can't see crap through those windows." He scanned the wash a last time. "Go now!" he cried, ducking his head.

Billy Red Clay jumped out and crouched behind the right front fender, with Thomas and Charlie close behind, each of them taking a position behind the truck's bed. Harley reached across to the glove box and retrieved his .38 before crawling out and dropping to the ground between Charlie and Thomas. He whispered to Charlie, "I don't believe Billy Moon was the driver. The seat is back way too far for a woman her size to be the driver."

Charlie took a moment to process this information, before quietly saying to the others, "That doesn't mean there's not two of them. Cover me." The investigator eased back to the rear of the truck, staying low and peering across the pickup bed, revolver at the ready. At the tailgate, he paused and looked back at his friends, each on the alert and prepared to act. The investigator moved slowly in behind the Jeep and, staying below the window crossed to the other side. He cautiously peeked around to the front of the vehicle, verifying what he now felt to be a less dangerous scenario.

The big man was sitting on the ground, slumped back against the sloping side of the sandstone boulder. Charlie could hear only the slightest wheezing rasp as Tito Alvarez was forced to take another labored breath. Blood seeped from Tito's nose and mouth, though Charlie could see it had previously been a more generous flow.

Probably the man had been shot, but at this point there was no visible evidence of that. It was hard for the investigator to envision any other way a man such as Tito Alvarez could have been brought down. Especially by one lone assailant, which he prayed was all they were up against.

There was no one else in the Jeep. Waving a hand above the vehicle's top he signaled for the others to come on around.

The three of them eased around, guns in hand. They moved up behind Charlie, who was now at Tito's side, checking his pupils and pulse.

"How bad is he?" Thomas asked. "There's no keys in that Jeep. Either he has them on him, or he lost them coming back down."

"He's not doing very well, I'm afraid. He's lost a lot of blood, some of it internally, I suspect." Charlie half turned and looked back at the men. "Billy, how about you and Thomas take Harley's pickup and go back to the trading post. From there you should be able to call this in on the radio in *my* truck." The investigator had to stop and think for a moment. "I didn't notice if the trader had a phone or not. He may have a private phone in his living quarters. In any case I don't want this getting out until we know what we've got. Tell dispatch where we are and that we need a copter in here to retrieve a casualty. While you're at it, tell them there may be more than one." Charlie thought a moment. "Thomas can drive my truck back up here, so we'll have some communications. There's no telling what we'll find up at Glynda Benally's place."

Charlie told Harley he would be staying there with him in case a tracker was needed. In the meantime, the tracker moved over to help with the wounded Tito Alvarez.

The other two men left on the double, knowing it would take some time to get to the trading post. Billy could use the radio to request a helicopter and notify the

146

FBI. Thomas could bring the truck back, leaving the Tribal policeman at the trading post to guide Fred's forensic crew in when they arrived. Everyone knew they had a long night ahead of them.

As Thomas and his nephew roared off into the gathering dusk, Charlie continued to render first aid and asked Harley, to circle the immediate area, looking for some sign of what had happened here. After only a short time he was back.

Charlie glanced up as his friend joined him by the injured man.

"How's he doing?"

"About the same, I guess. His breathing's a little steadier, if anything. The man's God-awful tough, no doubt about that. He's hanging in there."

Harley sighed. "You can't imagine just how tough, Charlie. He wasn't shot here." Harley said this pointing to the top of the wash, "It seems he was shot somewhere up on top, and then drug himself down here, trying to get away from the shooter, I would guess. Do you know where he's hit?"

"In the back, lower shoulder, big caliber, apparently that one may have just nicked his lung. One shot caught him in the lower leg, didn't break any bones but did damage some muscle tissue. That's about all I can see, but it's enough to have killed the average man."

Harley stood. "I think I'd best head back up on top and see what's going on at Glynda Benally's place while we've still got some daylight left."

Charlie hesitated, thinking he should go along with him, not knowing what he might run into. "There really isn't much more I can do down here right now. The bleeding has stopped, and as I said he seems to be breathing better."

"I don't know, Charlie…it might be a good idea for you to stay here and gather some brush for a signal fire. That helicopter pilot may need some kind of beacon to guide him in down here. It's hard to tell how long it will be before that chopper shows up, not from what I've seen in the past."

The investigator nodded thoughtfully, then sighed heavily. "You're probably right, I just hate to see you go in up there alone not knowing what's waiting for you."

Harley grinned. "Don't worry about me, big guy. I can take care of myself."

The Legal Service's Investigator was well aware Harley Ponyboy could take care of himself. The man had proven that numerous times.

Charlie listened as Harley scrambled up the trail to the top of the wash. He was still wishing he'd gone with him even as the sounds of his going died away.

Later, gathering firewood along the edges of the dry wash bed, the investigator still entertained lingering doubts, even as he set about building a signal pyre. It would be fully dark soon—a signal fire might mean the difference between life and death for the wounded Tito Alvarez. Of this much, he was certain. *Considering the scope of the injuries involved, I doubt anyone else I know could have survived such an ordeal...if he does survive.*

~~~~~~~

It was more than two hours before Harley Pony-boy made his way back down the steep and rocky trail off the edge of the wash—it had been dark for more than an hour by then. Charlie could hear him coming some distance out. As quiet as Harley was, when need be, he now was coming in such a way the investigator knew at once there was no longer any danger from that quarter.

Approaching the small fire Charlie had built against one end of the boulder, the tracker stared at the still form of Tito Alvarez. Harley's first words were, "Is the signal fire ready? I could see the running lights of the helicopter from up on top—probably not more than fifteen minutes from touch down."

Charlie glanced at the wounded man, "I'll light the fire. They can land in that wide spot in the wash to pick him up. I was just waiting to hear from you. I didn't want the signal fire to alert anyone else who happened to be up top. If this is the hospital's new medivac unit, it can only take one person at a time."

"Charlie, that woman up there is dead…she can wait if that's the case." He cursed under his breath as though blaming himself. "Too bad we didn't get here a little earlier. There's no sign up there of Rupert Kly or his truck. After tangling with Tito, I'm guessing he high-tailed it back through the Chuskas toward the family camp." Harley moved to the fire and held his hands out to the meager blaze. A breeze out of the north brought a night chill along with the pungent smell of sage off the flats across the wash. Looking over at Tito he saw that Charlie had placed his own coat over the man, leaving himself with very little to ward off the cold.

As the signal pyre struggled into flame, the distant whirl of the chopper's blades cut through the silence, apparently making its way straight down the wash. Moments later they listened as it changed course slightly to line up with the fire. Making a reconnaissance pass, it circled and came down in the exact place Charlie expected. He and Harley were waiting to lead the rescue party to the wounded man. Seeing the size of him, the stretcher bearers were relieved when the two Navajo quickly moved to take one end of the load.

After the helicopter lifted off, Charlie and Harley Ponyboy threw sand on the already dying signal fire, and then moved over into the shelter of the boulder at the edge of the wash. Harley kicked up the smaller fire, and the two stood warming themselves as they settled in to wait. It would be a while before Thomas would make it back with the truck.

While Charlie now had his coat back on, he had taken a chill and was trembling despite the warmth of the fire. "Did you have any trouble finding the *hogan* up there?"

Harley seemed lost in thought and took a minute, as if to organize his recollection of what he'd found up on top. "No trouble," he said, "there was a little daylight left and that helped some. Looked to me like a poor place to live. There must be a small spring somewhere though. I couldn't see it, of course, but there was no water barrel or easy way of hauling water back in there. So, I'm guessing there was a spring. I saw an old truck that looked to be in pretty good shape… the tire tracks leading up to the *hogan* looked fresh…probably made earlier this morning. The woman must have already been gone before Rupert got there this morning. He was probably waiting for her to come back."

Charlie knew his friend was taking his time getting around to Glynda Benally and didn't push him. Though he was anxious to know the details. He let him go at his own pace, knowing how he felt dealing with the dead, and not knowing how long it might take to find someone to do a cleansing ceremony.

Finally, however, Harley gave a shiver and began speaking of what had apparently taken place up at the *hogan*. "As I said there was still a little daylight left when I got there. I could see that Tito Alvarez had made it as far as the clearing and was in the brush shelter when someone hiding out beyond the camp shot him. The first shot must have been the one that hit him in the leg. I could see blood where he was dragging his left leg as he made for the *hogan*. There was blood up high on the door so he must have made it at least that far before taking the round in the shoulder. Once he was inside, there was a good amount of blood around where he rested on the floor. I think the shooter must have been unnerved he was still on his feet as he went into the *hogan*. Not knowing if Tito had a gun or not, he may have got scared and made a run for it, probably thinking someone hit that bad, should eventually bleed out anyway. When I went into the *hogan,* I could see where Alvarez tried to tie a makeshift tourniquet around his leg to staunch the bleeding and maybe let his wounds close some—

probably wanting to be sure the shooter had left, too. I'm guessing he then decided to try to make it back to the Jeep and drive back to town on his own." Harley made a face at the monumental task the man had set for himself. "His back-trail was not hard to follow until it became a little too dark. He got into the undergrowth and crawled for the better part of a half-mile through the sage—sometimes half-limping along on his feet—and sometimes on his hands and knees as he tried to work his way down here. He must have had a very hard time where the trail pitched off into the wash.

"And what about Glynda? Was she shot as well?"

Harley sighed and nodded. "She was, and at close range too, but obviously earlier than Alvarez. It looked to me like she had been dead for several hours. There was a sack of groceries still sitting on the table that hadn't been opened or put away. They may have been from the trading post but could have been from town…should she have left early enough. The shooter was obviously waiting for her."

Charlie mulled this over for a minute or so… "The trader or his wife didn't say anything about her being in the trading post that morning, did they?"

"No, but then they probably wouldn't have. I think they were already suspicious of me trying to find where she lived."

Charlie nodded, moving in closer to the fire and throwing on what was left of the dry sage. "Well, if Glynda did go into town this morning it might explain how Billy Moon found out where the woman lived. It makes me wonder what she would have to talk to Billy about in the first place. Tito could have overheard the conversation, I suppose, and then followed her home. He seemed to be pretty good at that sort of thing. I suppose it's also *possible* Billy Moon sent him out there. I hope she didn't send Alvarez expecting him to find Rupert Kly."

"I don't know either, Charlie but I remember you mentioning how odd you thought it was that Glynda and Rosemary were such good friends." Harley shook his head. "Of course, back in the day it wasn't uncommon for a *Diné* to have two or more wives, and I have heard those women often got along well with each other."

Charlie agreed. "No doubt there are things going on in the more isolated areas of the reservation most of us know nothing about, even today."

The two men talked on, trying to stay warm, and waiting on Thomas to return with Charlie's truck. He was certain the young liaison officer would have, by now, notified Fred Smith.

It stood to reason the bureau would send someone out with their forensics people to investigate the attempted murder of Tito Alvarez and death of Glynda Benally. One thing for certain: The Federal Bureau of Investigation would not want the crime scenes touched until they got there and oversaw the procedure."

It was only moments later they heard the distant grind of a laboring engine that told them Thomas was coming. The two men immediately put out the fire and began gathering their gear, preparing for the long ride back to town.

10

The Investigation

It was early afternoon when Charlie Yazzie and Tribal Officer Billy Red Clay arrived back in town, both men exhausted and wanting nothing more than a few hours sleep. Charlie dropped Billy off at his apartment, and then headed straight home to clean up and have something to eat before running back by the office. He had contacted Arlene on the radio coming in, to call the impound lot and let them know a tow truck would be hauling in Billy Moon's Jeep. He intended to follow through on that. Thomas Begay, got out of Harley's truck at Legal services. Then he too, headed home for some well-deserved rest.

When Charlie radioed ahead to check in, Arlene patched him through to his wife letting her know he was on his way home. He knew Sue would have something in the oven for him and, of course, would want to know all about what happened up in the Chuska's. After a quick nap he intended to drop by the hospital to see for himself how Tito Alvarez was doing. When he called, the nurse on duty told him the man was stable following surgery. Doctors diagnosed his condition as serious and his prognosis would be uncertain for the next 8 to 10 hours. In truth, Charlie couldn't imagine what was holding the man up. It still bothered him not knowing how or why Tito managed to reach Glynda Benally's place before he himself could get there. He had theories but nothing he could back up with any certainty.

~~~~~~~~

The next morning the Legal Services Investigator, having overslept, awoke to find himself alone in the house and a still a little bewildered. When the fog cleared, he remembered Sue saying she had to pick up Sasha at an after-school activity and dinner would be late.

The short drive to the hospital in Farmington put Charlie in the back parking lot just as visiting hours commenced. He doubted Tito Alvarez would be on the visitor's list this soon but decided he might yet wrangle a way in via his badge, should the man be conscious or have any sense of awareness. A nurse at the ICU desk, told Charlie the doctor left orders no one should be allowed in to see the man. Charlie, nevertheless, made his spiel about Legal Services having an interest in Tito—finally convincing the nurse to allow him to stay on the off chance Alvarez should come around and be able to identify who shot him. As he left the reception area, the nurse called him back and held up a set of keys with a dealer tag still attached. "The prep team in OR found these and someone remembered the rescue leader saying the reporting officer was looking for them."

Pocketing the elusive keys, he continued down the hall toward the waiting area. Charlie thought he recognized the two voices up ahead. Entering the waiting room, he was surprised to see Agent Fred Smith in an animated conversation with Billy Moon. The woman, speaking in a calm voice looked up as he came in and raised her eyebrows. Charlie smiled a greeting as he joined them.

The FBI man spoke first. "Ahh, Charlie, I called your home earlier and no one answered. You must have already been on your way here."

Charlie nodded at the two. "Probably so… Either that…or I was still asleep." Turning to Fred he asked, "So, how is Mr. Alvarez doing?"

"The nurse at the desk had just come on duty when we got here and didn't have much information…except no visitors were allowed in to see him."

Billy Moon nodded grimly. "No, and we haven't heard anything since yesterday. Earlier, Agent Smith called to inform me of what happened and offered to bring me into the hospital. It seems the doctor is tied up on another emergency but will talk to us as soon as he's free. That's about the extent of what we know for now."

Fred added, "I have an agent and forensics people on the way into town with the remains of Glynda Benally. Hopefully, we'll have a little more information when we hear from them. Since the Benally woman's death was obviously not due to natural causes, the medical examiner went along with them. Our agent has had a full day, what with interviewing the people at the trading post on his way back into town, and then questioning the recovery team here at the hospital. He's working up a report as we speak. Officer Billy Red Clay has already made his report, which I have yet to go over. That's about where we stand right now. I would like to hear what Harley Ponyboy has to say about his part, but that can wait until tomorrow."

Charlie inquired about the status of Billy Moon's Jeep, knowing the woman was basically without transportation.

Fred nodded. "Forensics examined the Jeep and released it to a tow truck driver to bring in sometime this afternoon."

They all turned to the door as a male voice was heard, "Sorry to keep you folks waiting…we had another little emergency to deal with." A tall, no-nonsense man who appeared to be in his early forties, the doctor introduced himself, and coming right to the point, said, "I've looked in on Mr. Alvarez and have gone over his most recent chart entries. It appears his vital signs are looking slightly better this morning. I expect him to rest easier as time goes on. He may possibly even be awake by this evening." He shook his head. "Though I can't assure you he'll be able to answer any questions by then. The injuries were quite serious, more so than first presumed. Our surgeon on duty did a truly remarkable job of repairing the internal damage. During the procedure however, the presence of a rather large tumor was discovered, something the patient probably wasn't aware of. It had metastasized and in the surgeon's opinion, was likely inoperable."

Billy Moon, clearly shocked at this revelation, threw the others an agonized glance. Obviously, the woman was deeply affected by the news. Her eyes filling with tears, she turned and looked away for a moment.

Fred was first to speak. "Doctor, is there no chance of me seeing him later this evening?

"No, I'm afraid not." The doctor assumed an expression which, seemed to convey a certain measure of sympathy. "We'll have an around the clock watch on him tonight and if you'll give the desk a call in the morning, they'll update you on his condition." The doctor adjusted his spectacles and offering a look of concern, lifted his clipboard in a gesture of farewell as he backed out of the room.

Fred glanced over at Charlie with an irritated frown. "Well, it looks like tomorrow then. Living here in Farmington, I'm the logical one to run by here in the morning…me, or the new agent who's working the case. Assuming he's able to get up in time to make visiting hours." Fred frowned. "I'm not sure how early I'll be up myself."

Charlie shifted his gaze to Billy Moon and said, "I can drop you off on my way home, Billy, if that's all right with you. No need in Fred having to drive all the way out to Shiprock and back into town again tonight."

Billy nodded. "I would appreciate that, Charlie. I know Fred has gone beyond the call already."

Fred answered that with, "In that case, I'll be on my way home to what I hope will be a good night's sleep." He glanced over his shoulder and saluted the investigator with a raised hand on the way out.

On the drive back into Shiprock, Billy Moon appeared lost in thought, speaking only when spoken to and even then, with as few words as possible.

"Billy, I'll have one of my people pick up your Jeep this afternoon and deliver it out to your coach. Officer Red Clay said the folks at the hospital found the keys with Tito's personal effects, and I picked them up for you. I figured you'd likely be needing a vehicle."

Billy shook her head as though rechanneling her thoughts in his direction. "That was very kind of you, Charlie, I've been in a bit of a daze since hearing of Rosemary's death. I know you may have been thinking I, or Tito, might have had something to do with that." She looked him straight in the eye. "Nothing could be farther from the truth. I assure you. Rosemary was the only friend I had when living with the Kly family. There was nothing she could do about the abuse that went on…she knew Rupert would kill her if she interfered. Still, she did what she could and even encouraged me to escape should I get the chance. She only had fourteen dollars to her name the night I left but insisted I take it with me. I'll never forget…the bus ticket was eleven dollars. I had three dollars left when I got off the bus in Albuquerque." She peered into the darkness as a tear ran down her cheek. "If it hadn't been for Rosemary, I might never have made it out of that mess."

Charlie shifted uncomfortably in the seat, and gripping the steering wheel a little tighter, asked the question that had been preying on him. "Billy, what happened to the baby you left behind up there?"

Her body stiffened in the seat beside him as she turned a stony gaze his way.

"How did you know about that, Charlie? Even I don't know what happened to that baby…or even if it was a boy or girl. Later, I found out right after I left, the whole family picked up and moved far back into the Chuskas. That was where Rupert Kly was from originally. I never heard from any of those people again. That is, until I got a note from Glynda Benally. The woman left it here with Tito when I was out getting groceries. The message said she'd had word from Rosemary, who told her she was going to Shiprock to talk to me. Glynda said it was only later she heard Rosemary was dead."

Billy hesitated a moment before going on. "Glynda mentioned Rupert would be at her place the next day…and that he seemed afraid of what I might do if I managed to find him. The last thing Rosemary told her, she said, was 'Billy Moon would, at last, rid them of the man's evil.' Glynda knew then she had to get a message to me no matter the cost. Sadly, it apparently cost her life." Billy settled back into the seat and turned to fix the Legal Services Investigator with a look of anguish mixed with hope.

"You know something, don't you, Charlie?"

"I think I might, Billy, not for sure, you understand, but I have a strong gut feeling about it. It wouldn't be fair to say more, but I'm looking into it and should know in a day or two." Charlie ducked his head and glanced out the side window as fence posts shimmered by in the reflected glow left behind by the headlights.

Out of the corner of his eye he could see Billy had her head turned toward him and was studying him as one would a stranger. He didn't sense any animosity in her gaze but there was something there he couldn't figure out.

A mile or more down the road, Billy still hadn't taken her eyes off him. "Why did you tell me this, Charlie, not knowing for sure?" Why would you say anything at all?"

Charlie thought long and hard before answering. It was a question he had already been asking himself. "Billy, I suppose it was because... I know how close you are to doing something that can't ever be undone. If that should happen, you might not be around to know something you have longed for most of your life."

"Charlie. I—"

Charlie held up a hand. "There's one other thing I think you should know. Fred Smith is shadowing your every move...and he is very good at it. The Bureau wants Rupert Kly...no matter what...and so do I. But make no mistake, Fred will be obliged to take you down instead should you be involved in any attempt on your uncle's life. Billy, I would hate to see so foolish a thing as revenge, destroy the sort of rewarding life you may yet have ahead of you."

Billy Moon hung her head as the tears began to flow. Nothing was said for the next new few miles but when at last she turned to him it was with a brighter vision for the future than she had ever dared imagined.

Charlie nodded as he glanced over at her and said, "Let Fred and me handle this, Billy. "We're very close now. And this time, we'll have the evidence that can put this man away for the rest of his life."

At Billy's tour bus, Charlie asked for the key and going inside, checked the rig from front to back. Coming back out he advised Billy to keep the door locked until his people delivered her Jeep back to her the next morning.

"I'll meet you back at the hospital just before visiting hours. I'm sure Fred will be there as well. Everything is going to be all right, Billy." Secretly, he hoped Tito's condition would, indeed, be improved, possibly even to the point he could identify his would-be assassin. This alone would give them a dead lock on the case. Yet, even without the attempted murder charge, the investigation into the deaths of Rosemary and Glynda Benally should lead to an almost certain conviction. There was a mountain of unmined evidence to sort through in these two deaths, not the least of which, was the anxiously awaited autopsy reports.

~~~~~~

On the drive into the hospital the next morning, Charlie first put in a radio call to Officer Billy Red Clay's dispatcher and had the call patched to the man's home phone. When Red Clay answered, Charlie surprised him with his request. "Billy, is there any chance you could do me a favor on your way into the office this morning?"

"You know I will if I can… What is it, Charlie?"

"I need for you to drop by the *Diné Bikeyah*, I figured you might be headed that way for coffee."

"Uh, actually, yes, that was my plan."

"Irene Nez…can you let me know if she is back to work this morning, and if not, what has happened with her…why she hasn't been in, and where she is?"

For a moment there was silence on the other end. "Do you mind me asking why that's important this morning, Charlie?"

"I just need to know her whereabouts. She's not in any trouble that I know of... I'll explain what's going on later. I'd rather not discuss it over the radio."

"Well, that's what I was going out there for this morning anyway, so will do."

"Thanks, Billy. I'll catch up with you. Maybe we can get together for lunch later today?"

Disconnecting from the call, the investigator sighed as he sat back in his seat and took time to consider the events of the previous day in a calmer, more ordered fashion. It was now obvious how Billy Moon learned the whereabouts of Rupert Kly. Still, he had to wonder if Billy purposely sent Tito Alvarez out there to confront the man, or if Tito had somehow taken it upon himself? These weren't the only unresolved questions that needed clearing up this morning. He was sure Senior Agent Fred Smith would have similar questions of his own he would want answered. And, in addition to these things, there still was the problem of Irene Nez *aka* Irene Kly. As far as Charlie was concerned, it seemed indisputable the young waitress, Irene, was Billy Moon's lost daughter. Irene's remarkable resemblance to the famous singer was irrefutable.

As he pulled into the hospital parking lot Charlie had to smile, thinking of how taken Officer Red Clay was with Irene. Surprisingly, he still hadn't put Irene and Billy Moon together. Even though the policeman had met the woman at the dinner party, the internationally known entertainer left him so star-struck it never entered his mind this local waitress could be related. But why would he think so? He didn't know what Thomas knew about the girl and had never seen Billy Moon when she was Irene's age. *No, Billy Red Clay was in for a rude awakening, hopefully, in a good way.*

Inside the hospital, Charlie stopped at the reception desk to inquire on the status of Tito Alvarez but was told the doctor had still not released his report. Instead, he was directed to the waiting area to await an update from the physician himself. Though early, he was still surprised to be the only one there so far. He'd imagined Smith would have beat him to the hospital for sure. Going to the window overlooking the parking lot, the investigator watched as an errant gust picked up a swirl of late autumn leaves. Then transforming itself into a miniature tornado, lofted its multihued passengers higher than the building—leaving them hanging a moment before releasing a vibrant shower over the parking lot. It was then he noticed the bright display engulf Billy Moon's Jeep. The woman stepped out and into a cascade of autumn leaves. Holding up her open hands to receive them, she laughed. Spotting the Investigator in the upper window, she smiled broadly, waving like a schoolgirl. Charlie smiled back, charmed by the innocent gesture and now even more assured in Billy's newfound sense of the future.

He turned as the waiting room door swooshed open as Fred Smith walked in.

"I thought maybe you'd slept in," Charlie offered as a greeting. "You must have parked out front."

"I did, I needed to pick up a copy of the Alvarez admission report from the Records Department. We're still early I see."

"Yes, Billy Moon is on her way up. She parked in the side lot."

"But no sign of the doctor as yet?"

"Not yet...Doctors, are always busy people, it seems?"

"I suppose so. I was told downstairs the doctor in question is in a conference concerning the patient's latest x-rays, taken early this morning. I would have thought that would have been done when he came in. But maybe these are just a follow up." Fred glanced at the door. "I expect we'll hear shortly." The Agent was about to say more but forestalled that notion as they heard footsteps coming down the hall.

Billy Moon, dressed in a casually stylish fall ensemble, was still breathing hard from taking the back stairs. A habit Charlie thought she may have picked up from her years fending off unwanted recognition. The woman seemed confident there would be good news but grew more serious as she learned there was no up-date on Tito's prognosis, and that additional x-rays had been required.

Fred related what he had been told downstairs, which she acknowledged with a further tightening of an already strained expression.

Understandable under the circumstances, Charlie thought. The three stood for a moment without speaking, and then found chairs as a Navajo family entered and seated themselves in a group at the far side of the room, traditional *Diné* by their dress and demeanor.

Billy Moon cast side glances at the people from time to time, perhaps hoping to recognize someone. Charlie wondered if she was looking for someone she'd once known, or more likely, someone she might have some intuitive connection to. The little group seemed not to notice or even look the woman's way, which would be the expected *Diné* response in such a situation.

Just as Fred Smith stood to go in search of further information, a doctor appeared, but went directly to the

Navajo family, who in turn, rose as though he was the person they had been waiting for.

Charlie Yazzie thought to himself, *well it* is a *doctor but apparently not 'the' doctor*. After a few minutes of consultation, this doctor led the stoic family to the person they had come to see.

On the way out the young clinician paused at the door and turned back to the three as though recalling something. "Oh, Doctor Granger will be in to see you folks in just a minute or so, he said he's been running behind but is on his way up here in just a few moments."

Agent Smith nodded his thanks and eyed the other two as he raised his eyebrows at the departing physician. "About time, I'd say." He managed a smile at the hopeful look on Billy Moon's face.

Charlie rose and shrugged a time or two to forestall the tightness he felt coming on in his shoulders. He looked toward the door just as the eagerly awaited older doctor hove into sight. Oddly enough, Charlie had never heard anyone mention his name before, or if they had, he'd forgotten it. *Something that seems to be more common now that I'm forty.* He immediately noticed the doctor, unlike their previous meeting, was frowning. Billy Moon noticed it too and frowned in return.

Doctor Granger was indeed the same physician they'd spoken to the day before and appeared to be running to form. Clutching his clipboard in one hand he didn't dilly-dally but came right to the point. "Well, we have some good news and a little not so good. First and foremost, Mr. Alvarez appears wide awake this morning, yet still seems unable to muster the power of speech." The doctor sniffed a time or two as he consulted his clipboard, as though to confirm his own prognosis, then looked up. "Often in these cases, improvement comes in rather small increments—not all at once, and certainly not as quickly as we might wish. The bottom line is, while the patient *has* physically improved since last evening, he still seems unable to communicate." The good doctor hesitated, "There is the possibility he's just disinclined to speak, I'm leaning in that direction."

Billy's mouth relaxed a little as she nodded. "Doctor, I wonder if I might speak privately to Tito? We are very old friends, and I may be able to entice him, if he's at all capable of communicating." A look crossed the doctor's face that could only be interpreted as a 'no.'

Billy instantly countered with a reproach of her own. Crossing her arms, she fixed the physician with a cold and calculating gaze. "You may not be aware of it, Doctor, but I am the one taking care of *all* of Mr. Alvarez's current medical expenses." She shook her head sadly, saying, "The poor man has neither money, nor insurance, of any kind."

In light of this new information, the doctor cleared his throat a time or two, and then after a momentary pause, allowed as how a few minutes might not hurt. Turning, he indicated Billy was to follow him, and without looking back, left for Tito's room.

Charlie and the FBI agent stood looking at one another. "What do you think, Fred?"

Fred touched the tip of his tongue to his upper lip and moved it back and forth a few times as if in contemplation. "I think we are never really going to know what goes on in that room, regardless of what Alvarez says or doesn't say."

Charlie considered this for a moment but could only partially agree. "Maybe, Fred, but then again, maybe not. In any case, I have an important call to make and will get back to you as soon as possible." Giving a push of his chin towards Tito's room, the investigator murmured, "Hopefully by then, we may know more about what happens in there."

Downstairs, Charlie sat in his truck trying to figure out where he should go from here with Billy Moon. There was no doubt in his mind she would get the man to talk. Picking up the two-way mic he called the Tribal police dispatcher. Again, he asked to be patched through to Billy Red Clay's mobile unit.

The policeman came on in a burst of static, and Charlie reached for the squelch knob in an effort to navigate that almost impossible adjustment between clarity and chaos. Suddenly, Billy came through clear as a bell "...You there, Charlie? ...You there? Over!"

"Yes, Billy, where are you?"

"I'm sitting outside the *Dinébikeyah,* waiting for you to call. I just had breakfast inside. Irene is not back at work. They said she had a call from the trading post, saying there'd been a death in the family. I guess she didn't think about calling in to work, just took off to be with them. Her people don't have a phone, so she's been out of touch these last couple of days."

"What did her boss have to say about her taking off without any notice, Billy? Your Uncle Thomas thinks they'll fire her when she comes back."

"No. Surprisingly enough, when the old lady that runs the place heard what happened, she said nothing about firing her."

The sound of an ambulance wailed in the background. "Listen, Charlie, just before your call broke through someone reported a wreck out on 64. I'm going to have to get on out there. There's a patrolman on the

174

scene but he needs help—I'll talk to you when I get back in town. Over!"

This was not what Charlie wanted to hear concerning Irene and her whereabouts, leaving him in somewhat of a quandary as what to say to Billy Moon. Though he was convinced the girl was her daughter, convincing the woman of that might prove a little harder without any real proof. He had counted on introducing Irene in the flesh, making their relationship hard to deny.

The investigator was still sitting in the hospital parking lot when Billy Moon hurried out. Fred Smith was not with her. That alone was cause for conjecture. Getting out of the truck Charlie waved and headed toward her Jeep.

Billy Moon appeared not to notice him and opening the door, got into her vehicle, only rolling down the window as the investigator approached. Her face was drawn and pale. The woman didn't meet his gaze and started the engine before saying, "I can't talk right now Charlie, something's come up that won't wait. I'll let you know what's going on when I know more."

"You talked to Tito…?"

"Yes." Putting the Jeep in gear she accelerated past him, without another glance.

Charlie, raising a hand in question, could only stand silently, mouth slightly ajar as the Jeep roared onto the street.

Coming out of the hospital Fred Smith hailed the investigator as he too watched the Jeep speed away from the parking lot. Charlie met him on the sidewalk. The FBI man shook his head. "I was tied up on the phone when she hustled past me in the reception area. I'm assuming she didn't say anything about how it went…with Tito, I mean?"

"I asked her if he talked…"

"And…?"

"She said, yes…that was pretty much it."

Fred looked up at a clear and sun-drenched sky and sighed. "Looks like it's going to be a nice day."

11

The Grind

Harley Ponyboy and Thomas Begay were leaning on the rails of the Yazzie's corral. The top rail was a stretch for Harley, but Thomas seemed to find it comfortable enough. After pitching a few forkfuls of hay over the fence, the two laughed as the mare turned her rear to Charlie's gelding and kicked at him, pushing him off the feed. The two men talked back and forth, arguing the merits of the two horses while keeping an eye out for the investigator. Charlie was due home from work any time and the pair had it timed about right—they didn't have long to wait. Spotting the man pull up to the mailboxes at the end of the lane, Harley nudged the tall Navajo in the ribs and pointed his chin in that direction. "There he is... Right on time."

"Yep, dependable old' Charlie, you can always count on the man to be where he's supposed to be." The two nodded at each other, agreeing for the first time that day. As the truck drew nearer Thomas peered more closely at the driver. "He doesn't look all that happy, does he?"

Harley squinted slightly in the glare off the truck's windshield and chuckled—for the second time that day he was obliged to agree. "He has his rear in the air over something, alright." The old *Diné* expression alluded to a skunk whose ire had been raised and was on the fight.

As the truck swerved in beside them the men stood back a little to avoid having their toes run over. The passenger side window was down, and Charlie grimaced, saying, "Now what?

Thomas was grinning. "We already fed your horses just so you'd have a little extra time to chat."

The investigator frowned at the men. "About what?"

"Oh, this and that…We haven't seen much of you since that little dust-up down-country. We were just wondering how that big fella in the hospital was doing, that's all." Harley was smiling as he said this and didn't bother to change expression as he waited for a reply.

"Well, your guess is as good as mine—he's alive, if that's what you mean—but other than that I don't know a damn bit more than the two of you, and that's a fact."

It wasn't often they heard the man talk in so loose a fashion and found it refreshing. Thomas smirked and looked away. Harley, undaunted, laughed outright and said, "I think Sue is looking to talk to you, too. I see her peeking out the kitchen curtains every now and then."

Charlie glanced up at the house and drew his brows together in a tightknit scowl. "I'll swear, I don't know how women think. First Billy Moon won't talk and now Sue has something to say and won't say it." He stepped down from the truck and moved alongside them, seeing for himself how much they had fed the two horses. Sue was particular about her mare. He nodded grudgingly and looked the two over. "Neither one of you working today?"

Thomas paused a moment, saying finally, "Not so anyone would notice, we're not. Professor Custer hasn't had anything going on of late—and he's about the only one either of us cares to work for anymore."

Charlie couldn't help frowning. "Well, I suppose that stands to reason, doesn't it?" Leaving his truck parked where it was, the three walked up to the house, stomping the dust off their boots on the porch before going in.

Sue saw them coming and had coffee cups already set out and a fresh pot on the stove. There was a plate of freshly baked cinnamon rolls from a recipe she had been experimenting with. The three sat themselves at the table leaving a seat open for her, which she ignored as she poured their coffee.

"You're not going to have a cup with us?" Charlie could sense she was in a mood and felt it best not to press her.

Sue stood a moment, arms crossed, and tapping a foot. "Billy Moon called a few minutes ago and wants you to meet her at the cafe in the morning about eight o'clock. She wants to talk."

"Oh, so now she wants to talk, does she?" Charlie glanced grimly at the other men, as though confirming their earlier conversation.

Sue eyed all three of them. "I don't think she wanted to say anything around Agent Smith."

"Why didn't she drop by the office or leave a message?"

"Well, Charlie, maybe she needed a little time to think, or was busy herself. It's not like she has a phone line strung out to that bus, you know."

The other two men, feigning disinterest in the exchange, remained in silent contemplation—Harley gazing out the kitchen window—while Thomas was eyeing the fresh rolls. Both had known the couple for years and were close enough not to be embarrassed by the conversation…or by being excluded from it.

The investigator rubbed his forehead in thought, saying in a more conciliatory tone, "I'll drop by the cafe in the morning and see what she's thinking." The other two men remained quiet as they helped themselves to the baked goods, while nodding their approval, Sue wouldn't have put them out there if she hadn't meant for them to have one or two. Charlie regarded his two friends with a speculative glance and nearly missed the roll Harley tossed to him.

~~~~~~~~

The breakfast rush was almost over and the *DinéBikeyah's* parking lot was little more than half-full. An oilfield work-over rig still took up most of the side lot, leaving Charlie a tight space among a gaggle of company trucks parked in front. He couldn't help thinking it odd Billy Moon now saw fit to meet him in so public a place, if what she had wanted in the first place was privacy.

Shaking his head, the investigator moved toward the door just as a group of oilfield hands came straggling out, primed to get on with yet another day's work. The oil and gas industry wasn't as busy as once it had been—depending more on work-over rigs and fracking jobs to carry them through the slow time. It occurred to him, *Nowadays, nearly half the crews are either Navajo or Ute—good for the reservation economy—no matter what your politics were.* Change had always come slowly for the *Diné,* but there was little doubt now it had snuck up on them. He hoped he would be around to see how it turned out. If not, his children surely would.

Charlie hadn't seen Billy Moon's Jeep in the parking lot and chose a booth at the back near the rear window. Not private, but out of the morning traffic and quiet enough for a conversation.

As he seated himself, he turned over the inverted coffee cup while gazing out the window at the workover rig parked just outside, watching as the driver entered the cab and started the big diesel. Pulling out of the lot onto a secondary road the rig was followed by two of the company pickups from out front. One of the Navajo drivers noticed him at the window and raised a casual two finger salute in passing. Charlie returned the gesture just as he heard the waitress coming up. Turning from the window, he was surprised to see Irene Nez, a raised eyebrow posing a question as she stood holding the steaming pot.

"Well, hello, I thought that was you I saw coming in. Where's your friend Billy Red Clay this morning?"

The young woman wore rather a wan smile but otherwise seemed chipper enough. Glancing at his watch, Charlie nudged his cup to be filled. "I expect he'll be along when he goes on break." He glanced at his watch. "Probably in about an hour or so… I'm sure he will be happy to see you are back on the job."

Irene nodded as she poured. "I guess I'm lucky to still have a job to come back to."

"How so?"

"I got called away for a death in the family. It was late at night, so I didn't call in—that was a mistake I won't make again. What can I get you this morning, Investigator?"

"Actually, I'm expecting one more…so if you can hold up until then, I'd appreciate it."

"Not a problem, I'll just leave a couple of menus and check back when I see your party come in."

Charlie nodded his thanks. *Well, I didn't see that coming. Billy Red Clay must not have known she was back, either, or I'd have already heard. Something must have come up.* He sat sipping his coffee as he wondered who Irene's family had lost. Now that Rosemary was gone, the only ones he could imagine would be Gladys and her husband Lester. Odd their last name was Nez, same as Irene's married name, but not really, given that Nez is one of the top twenty surnames on the reservation. According to early traders, those twenty names once made up over sixty percent of all *Diné* surnames. In any case Rosemary's daughter and husband were the only people she would likely care to see out there in the Chuskas.

As Charlie mulled these things over, he decided not to say anything to Billy Moon about Irene's almost certain connection to her…not just yet anyway. Not until he'd had time to think it through. The investigator had no more than determined this, when he saw the inimitable Ms. Moon making her way back to the table. She spotted him soon enough and smiled broadly as she raised a hand. He rose from his chair to greet her, keeping an eye out for Irene as he pulled out a chair for the rock star.

"Thanks, Charlie," she said sweetly. "I hope I haven't kept you waiting long." Billy was well turned out, as usual, and seemingly in a much better mood than the last time he saw her. "I suppose you are wondering what had gotten into me yesterday?"

Charlie shrugged in lieu of answering, allowing the woman to continue at her own pace.

Head canted to one side, Billy considered the investigator a moment before nodding her understanding. "It's just that I was so upset seeing Tito like that, not just the injuries, which were bad enough, but the news of the inoperable tumor. I've never seen him so vulnerable."

"You said he talked to you there in the hospital room. What exactly did he say, Billy?"

The woman sighed slowly and looked directly into his eyes. "Charlie, his voice was so weak I could barely understand him. He admitted taking the Jeep to see if he could locate Rupert Kly. Whenever he thinks something is a matter of security or my personal safety, he is apt to take things under his own advisement…and often without letting me know beforehand. He usually proves himself right, too, I'll say that for him." She looked past the investigator and murmured, "I think that's our waitress coming, isn't it?"

Charlie turned his head slightly and agreed. "That's her alright. She's an interesting girl, or so Billy Red Clay tells me. I think he's sort of sweet on her, if you know what I mean?"

"Well, I can certainly see why. She's a stunning young woman."

"You, she is, isn't she?" Charlie watched carefully for some sense of her thinking but saw little to base any sort of an opinion on.

Irene stopped by the coffee station for a fresh pot and was at the table before anything else could be said.

The investigator looked up and smiled, saying, "Ah, right on time, Irene. We are starving."

The young waitress smiled at Charlie and turned to pour a cup for Billy.

Turning up her cup, the woman studied Irene as she poured the steaming coffee. Billy glanced at the girl briefly, and then shot Charlie a look he couldn't quite figure out.

"Well, what will we be having this morning?" Irene asked brightly, staring at Billy as she stood poised with pad in hand. An odd little smile crossed her face for just an instant.

Without missing a beat, Billy Moon made her choice. "I believe I'll have the sausage and eggs…over medium on the eggs, and wheat toast. Hashbrowns will be fine."

Scribbling furiously, the girl looked up and said, "Got it," but kept eye contact a moment as though she might say something more. Then, turning to Charlie, who had been watching the pair, asked what he would have, then took his order as if on autopilot. As she left the table, the girl gave Billy a last bewildered glance before hurrying off with their orders.

"I think she may have recognized you—she seemed a little flustered. But I'll bet you get that all the time."

Unsmiling, Billy nodded. "It's when they don't recognize me, I'll know I have a problem." She took a sip of her coffee. "What did you say Irene's last name was, again?"

Charlie pursed his lips in thought. "I don't think I did say, Billy, but it's Nez…Irene Nez. I'm told she was married for a short time. A boy down in Gallup, I think it was. But it didn't last long, except for the name."

Billy smiled wryly. "I wouldn't hold that against her, Charlie. I've been down that road a time or two myself." She added a little cream to her cup, stirring the coffee a turn or two at a time as she peered across the table. "I get the feeling our conversation has taken a different turn here, Charlie. Am I right? I've noticed you do that occasionally—an interrogation technique possibly—part of your business?"

"If that's how I've come across, I am truly sorry. I hadn't noticed doing it. I'll keep that in mind."

"You said earlier you might have some conclusive word on my child, possibly even today."

"I did say that, and now that we've talked, I'm certain who she is.

"She? So, I have a daughter? Where is she then, Charlie?"

"I have a feeling you already know, Billy." The investigator glanced toward the kitchen. "She's on her way over with our breakfast right now." When he saw the look on Billy's face, he quickly assured her. "You don't have to say anything just yet. I know you need time to wrap your head around this, and God knows you'll want to figure out how you want to handle it. This isn't the time or place for her to formally meet her mother for the first time. When she gets off work in a couple of hours, I'll drop her off out at your place...if that's all right with you. The two of you can sort all this out in private for as long as it takes. I just thought you might like a heads-up."

Billy Moon sat totally still and, without the slightest sign of emotion, slowly nodded her head.

Charlie didn't know what he had expected. But it wasn't anything like this. The woman's depth of self-control was uncanny. A slight chill fell across him as he turned to see Irene standing there holding their breakfast tray. She could have been Billy twenty years ago. The girl began serving the food, all the while keeping her eyes fixed on Billy Moon, who remained remarkably calm, checking their orders as though it was her only concern.

"Is there anything else I can get you folks?" Irene said in a softly cautious tone."

"No, dear, everything looks very nice, and smells delicious, thank you."

Charlie smiled and nodded, which was about all he could put together at this point.

The two ate in silence for several minutes. "So, how long have you known?" Billy said this in a tone that might have hinted of a slight reproach.

Charlie ignored it. "Not long. It took a while for it to register at first, and then a little longer for it to sink in, I suppose. But it didn't take long to verify who she was. There were several people who remembered her and where she came from. I wanted to be completely certain in my own mind before saying anything."

Billy Moon considered this as she raised her cup, watching him over the rim as she took a long sip. "Well, you were almost too late."

The investigator had a pretty good idea what she meant by this but took it in stride. It was exactly what he had been thinking.

12

The Reunion

Heading back to the office Charlie worried he might have handled the meeting with Billy Moon rather badly. Admittedly, he had been a little put out with her refusal to offer up what she had learned from Tito Alvarez. And he was quite sure there had been more to it than what she'd told him. Yet, he hated to think he might have been too abrupt with the woman. Retribution was not a facet of who he was—at least he hoped it wasn't.

On his way out of the cafe, he caught up with Irene at the coffee station to tell her Billy Moon wanted to see her when she finished her shift. He'd told the girl; someone would pick her up at her apartment and take her out to the fairgrounds to meet the woman.

Though obviously bewildered by this, the girl agreed to go yet seemed anxious and somewhat mystified at the request.

Charlie thought the girl obviously had a lot of her mother in her, and hopefully she had inherited the same degree of self-reliance and inner strength.

Coming into town the investigator frowned as a rising breeze lifted a swirl of red sand and peppered the front of his truck. A pale crimson cloud was rolling down off the far ridges to the north, marring what had been an idyllic fall day. A likely portent of Autumn's long-winded slide into winter.

At some point, it occurred to him it might be wise to ask Officer Red Clay to deliver Irene to her mother. Probably best, in fact, for all involved. Irene trusted the young policeman and he, no doubt, would be more than happy to do it. *It might be explained as a security measure due to the woman's celebrity.*

Charlie certainly didn't feel the time was right for pressing Billy Moon for whatever she'd heard from Tito at the hospital. That would have to wait. Waiting too long, however, was near certain to cause Agent Smith to take over that responsibility himself. Charlie intended to hear firsthand what the woman had learned, thinking she might be less free with the Federal Agent.

At the office he called Billy Red Clay to fill him in on what had gone on at the cafe that morning. After the officer recovered from that shocker, he asked Billy to take Irene over to Billy Moon's tour bus at the fairgrounds. As anticipated, the officer instantly volunteered.

"Billy, I wouldn't tell her why Ms. Moon wants to meet or even offer to wait there for her. This will be a private and, I'm sure, a very emotional experience for both—and will probably take some time. I wouldn't be surprised if Irene winds up spending the night."

The policeman, still apparently reeling from news of the girl's relation to the celebrity, managed to say, "I understand, Charlie. I'll be…you know…discreet. I just hope this thing works out for the best; for Irene and her mother, I mean."

What Charlie figured he was really thinking was how this new information would affect his relationship with Irene. While it might well open an entirely new world for the girl—for Billy Red Clay, it would likely be a world where he had no place.

~~~~~~

Officer Red Clay glanced at Irene as they drove out to the fairgrounds, his heart thundering in his chest. Finding Billy Moon was her birth mother was bound to be a game changer for Irene. He grimaced to himself.

It was an entirely unexpected development in his attempt to win Irene over. An attempt he thought had been progressing quite well, until now.

As he let Irene off at her mother's tour bus, the young Tribal policeman was quick to point out the payphone, just across the way from the coach. "Irene, should you need anything at all, a ride or anything, feel free to give me a call." He handed her his card with home and office number.

Irene glanced at the card before slipping it in her pocket. "Thanks, Billy, I'm sure I'll be fine. But it's nice to know someone is looking out for me." She gave the young policeman a peck on the cheek and opened the car door. "I don't know what this is all about, but I'm sure any girl on the reservation would be happy to change places with me right now. It's not every day a girl like me gets to meet Billy Moon."

He frowned to himself and nodded. *If only you knew, Irene. If only you knew.*

~~~~~~

Billy Moon, watching from the window of the coach, met her daughter at the door and ushered her into an interior more luxurious than anything the girl might have imagined. Pointing to a seat on the couch and lifting her hands to the tastefully decorated interior, the woman smiled. "Well, what do you think of it?"

The girl appeared mesmerized as she slowly took it all in. Soft jazz played in the background as she ran her hand across the rich leather of the couch. "To be honest, I didn't know anyone lived like this…except in the movies, of course."

Billy laughed. "Just think of it as a house on wheels. For me, it's home. Just another part of the business I'm in. I guess you could say it's the only stable part of my life."

"And what an exciting life that must be, I can't even imagine how exciting."

Billy considered the sentiment in a somewhat guarded manner. "I suppose it has its moments, I'll grant you that. Yet, there has to be more to life than this, wouldn't you agree? The older I get the more certain I am of that. I think you'll understand what I mean, one day."

The girl nodded, despite not being wholly convinced.

Billy Moon smiled to herself. "What can I get you? Coffee, tea, a soda? I'd offer you a glass of wine, but we're not allowed to have that here on the reservation, are we?"

Irene smiled. "Not legally, I suppose, but it's not uncommon, and who will ever know? I'd love a glass of wine. It's been a long day."

"I'm sure it has. It might surprise you to know I've spent many a day waiting tables myself, and when I was exactly your age, too."

Irene laughed lightly. "Oh, and how would you know exactly how old I am, Ms. Moon?"

Billy Moon turned from the refrigerator to the sink in the process of twisting the cork from a bottle of cold Pinot Grigio. Tilting her head, she gave the girl a long searching look, and said in a husky voice. "Because I was there the night you were born."

Billy turned back to the refrigerator for chilled glasses. Bringing them to the coffee table, she smiled at the shocked look on her daughter's face. Sitting down she concentrated on filling the glasses. Glancing up, she nodded at the blank expression on the girl's face. "Yes, Irene, I'm your mother—I would have been here sooner if I was able, it just wasn't in the cards." She paused for only a moment. "Those are the little tricks life plays on us, right? We don't always get a square deal—right off the top of the deck."

Irene reached down, picked up her glass and downed it all in one long swallow. Taking a great gulp of air, she nearly choked, and in a barely audible voice asked. "Are you sure...?"

Billy chuckled as she turned to the backlit credenza behind her. Plucking a frame from the back of the shelf, she handed it to her daughter.

Irene took the photograph and stared at it for a long while. "This is like looking into a mirror. I knew this morning at the cafe I'd seen you somewhere, and now I know where."

Billy downed her own glass and, taking a deep breath, poured two more. "Well, it's a hell of a thing, isn't it? Meeting like this after all these years...and you a grown woman. I was beginning to wonder, myself, if I would ever see this day."

Irene looked around her as though in a daze. "Rosemary once told me my mother would someday come for me. I never really believed that would happen and now, here it is, just as she said. I don't know what to think."

"I expect we both have a lot to say to one another, and it's probably going to take a while to get that done. For one thing, I'd like to know everything about you and what's been going on in your life." Billy could see no sign of reproach or accusation in the girl's manner or in the forthright way she met her gaze. And this alone told her a great deal about her daughter and who she had become. To say she was pleased would be putting it mildly.

~~~~~~

That night at dinner Charlie Yazzie filled Sue in on all the details of the day, other than how everything turned out, of course. Neither he nor Billy Red Clay had heard any update on the reunion.

As Sue listened to the story, she came away from the stove and sat across from Charlie as he finished the tale. His wife's eyes were glistening, and she dabbed at them with the hem of her apron. "What an incredible story," she murmured. Sue reached across the table and touched her husband's hand. "You must feel a lot of satisfaction in being a part of their finding one another."

"Well, it was a combined effort, you know, of several people, a couple of whom gave their lives to right a very old wrong. Rosemary and the girl's other aunt were killed trying to help Billy Moon. God only knows how things will turn out for Tito Alverez. He was already a prime suspect in Rosemary's murder and possibly even the shooting of Glynda Benally. We still don't know what came about up there...not for sure. Even Harley Ponyboy said his idea of what happened could be way off base."

As Sue rose and moved to the stove to check on dinner, she thought she could smell something beginning to burn. She clicked on the exhaust fan just as the phone rang and looked back at the table. "Can you get that for me, Charlie? I'm sure it's Lucy...I can't leave this gravy...it's trying to scald. Just tell her I'll call her right back."

Charlie sighed and easing out of his chair, moved into the living room to answer away from the noise. When Sue had dinner back under control and had turned off the fan, she could hear her husband still on the phone. She knew immediately he wasn't talking to Lucy Tallwoman. Charlie came back in the room with rather a grave look on his face, voice heavy with emotion as he spoke. "That was Billy Red Clay. Someone just tried to snatch Irene Nez out at the fairgrounds."

"What...?"

Charlie took a deep breath. "She'd gone across the lot to phone Billy Red Clay to say she was spending the night with her mother and for him not to worry. Just as she was dialing him up, someone came up behind her

198

and tried to put her in a chokehold. She twisted away enough to start hitting him in the head with the telephone. She later said she could smell alcohol on the man. It was dark and he wore a black hooded sweatshirt. She couldn't see who it was. That's when Billy Red Clay came on the phone. He could hear the commotion and started shouting that 'she had reached Tribal police'. Apparently, the attacker heard enough and turned and ran off into the night. Billy jumped in his unit and was there in ten minutes. He alerted dispatch to patch him through to me here at the house as he drove. He's with the girl and her mother now. He has two other officers from Tribal on the way, and the situation appears to be in hand. He said they're going to leave one of the officers on duty there for the rest of the night. He and the other one are out scouring the neighborhood for the attacker. He'll check back in with me first thing in the morning. There's not a thing I can do out there tonight, and I'm sure he'll get back to me in the morning. He said he'd called Fred who planned to send someone out to take statements first thing in the morning."

Sue stood as if horror stricken, hands to her mouth in fear for the girl. Charlie wrapped an arm around her, as Sasha, hearing the ruckus, came from her bedroom wanting to know what was going on. Sue told her what

199

happened as their daughter pitched in to help save dinner.

Charlie, sitting back down at the table, watched as the pair filled plates and brought them over. He was still trying to mentally process Billy Red Clay's report. It had already occurred to him it could have been almost anyone hanging around the fairgrounds. A random coincidence unrelated to Billy Moon or Rupert Kly.

Before dinner was over the investigator fielded two more calls. One from Billy Red Clay, who had not discovered any trace of the perpetrator. The other call was from Thomas Begay who called to say his nephew phoned asking him where the fugitive may have gone. It wasn't the first time Billy Red Clay consulted with his uncle on criminal behavior—always in the strictest confidence, of course.

Often in tune to her husband's way of thinking, Sue ventured the question, "So, the FBI has no clue where this Rupert Kly is?"

"No, not as far as I've heard. I suppose he could be anywhere by now. I'm not sure Fred is giving the man enough credit. He may well be smarter than any of us know, and that could make him more dangerous than first reckoned. In any case, the longer it takes to bring him in…the less likely it will happen."

Sue nodded. "And you're thinking you need to be the one who goes after him?"

"Thomas already approached me. He thinks he and Harley and me should take a little jaunt up in the Chuskas and see if we can pick up his trail or at least ferret out some word of him. Or make certain he's left the country. Like Fred, Thomas thinks the man is still somewhere in the area."

"What do you think?"

"I think it's better than doing nothing—the FBI is not very effective in that country—and Kly could wind up killing someone else if he's not stopped."

"What's Fred going to think about you three mixing in? That's caused problems in the past."

"Fred's not like past Senior Agents. He's from here, knows the reservation, and understands the *Diné* and how they think—better than anyone else in the Bureau, I'll wager. I think privately he will welcome the help. And remember this, Billy Moon is a client of Legal Services, that puts her in my jurisdiction."

"Charlie, are you thinking this incident tonight was someone other than Kly?"

"There's always the chance it might have been a random attacker, a drunk or whatever. Maybe even Irene's ex-husband returned to do her some harm, anything's possible, I guess. I'm sure the Bureau will be working all the angles and they cast a wide net when it comes to this sort of thing." He drew a long breath. "I think Thomas is right. He and Harley and I had better go have a look up in the Chuskas and see where that leads."

Sasha Yazzie spoke for the first time. "Dad, now that you're forty, don't you think you might be getting a little old for chasing around the country after bad guys? You're supposed to be a lawyer, aren't you, Dad?"

The Legal Services investigator frowned as he watched Sue's face for some affirmation of their daughter's claim. Wearing the ghost of a smile his wife turned to the seventeen-year-old. "I'm sure your father has taken his age into account when considering how hard this little venture might be on him and his two elderly friends."

Sasha, being a chip off the female side of the old block, nodded curtly toward her father. "And has he considered the consequences of leaving behind an aging widow and beautiful orphaned daughter?"

Lately, Charlie had been amazed at how easily Sasha shifted into adult mode, when it suited her purpose. The girl had a biting wit and growing capacity for sly repartee. He would have to talk to her one of these days, should he find time to work up the courage.

Putting on a straight face the investigator held up a hand to signify the end of the conversation. Falling silent the little family managed to finish dinner, each convinced they'd made their point.

The investigator rose early the next morning and was in the kitchen making coffee when Sue came out in her bathrobe.

"What time are you going to leave?"

"As soon as Thomas gets here. I gave Harley a heads-up last night."

Nodding, the woman began breakfast without saying anything for several minutes. When she did it was in a calm and measured tone. "What do you think will happen now with Billy Moon and her daughter?"

"Well, that's a hard one to call. There's a nice RV park in Farmington. I'm sure the women would be more comfortable there. Not to mention being closer to the hospital and Tito Alvarez. They have phone hook-ups there now, too. She does after all, still have a business to run. But I don't think she'll leave the area. Not yet. She came here to settle a couple of old scores. Knowing her as I do now, I doubt she'll leave until she gets that opportunity."

"And her daughter? What do you suppose she'll do?"

"I wish I knew. Most likely it will depend on how the two of them worked things out last night. The girl has a small apartment and a job here. And, of course, there's Billy Red Clay. Only Irene knows how deep her feelings run when it comes to that situation."

"I can't imagine anything here on the reservation keeping the girl from the sort of life she'd have with her mother. Can you?"

Charlie shrugged but didn't have the opportunity to offer an opinion—interrupted by the rattle and grind of Thomas Begay's old diesel truck as it labored up the drive.

With a wry grin, Sue started making toast and frying bacon. *Lucy Tallwoman and I will have plenty to talk about this day.*

~~~~~~

Charlie Yazzie filled his gas tank after work the night before and now cautioned himself to keep a close eye on the gauge, knowing how easy it was to lose track. The journey might involve a serious number of miles, most of it in the backcountry. Harley Ponyboy sat in the middle allowing long-legged Thomas Begay to ride shotgun. There were lunches packed for each and several water bottles behind the seat.

They were barely out of town, when Billy Red Clay came on the two-way, letting Charlie know he had arranged his day off to help Billy Moon and her daughter take her tour bus into Farmington. He would help settle them in the RV park where they might feel safer. The woman told him she was perfectly capable of driving the big bus herself. Still, the young officer had insisted on coming along to help them set up. And to see for himself where they were located, and what security provisions might be available. The Tribal law officer wasn't quite ready to give up on Irene Nez, not just yet anyway.

Charlie had already figured Billy Moon for putting her rig in the RV park in town and thought it a wise move under the circumstances. The rock star was no stranger to living in chancy circumstances and knew how to play the odds. He smiled to himself thinking of the young cop's last words to him. "I will let the girl's mother know how things stand between Irene and me." Billy had decided to stand his ground.

Thomas listened to that conversation with a frown, later saying, "My nephew is making a mistake taking up with this girl. No good can come from it...not for him anyway. I've said it before; there's something not right with that woman."

"Billy Moon, you mean...how so?"

"I don't know how so, it's just a feeling I have. I don't know what it is."

Harley Ponyboy, sitting between the two, nodded wisely. "Me too, and I don't know what it is either."

Charlie sighed. "It's probably because she talks like a white person and grew up in an entirely different world. That's most likely what it is."

Harley grinned. "You talk like a white person, too. We don't get that feeling about you. Does she speak Navajo?"

"Surprisingly, yes, she does speak Navajo. Billy didn't leave the reservation until she was a teenager and according to Robert Hoskinny, the Kly family spoke only Navajo at home. She has a sharp mind and a good memory...maybe too good."

"What do you mean by that?" Harley guessed the investigator felt more comfortable around Billy Moon than either he or Thomas, but still he thought Charlie was missing something more sinister in the woman.

With a curious glance, Thomas turned to listen, and when Harley grew quiet, said, "You still think she wants to punish her uncle in her own way?"

"Something like that is weighing on her...that's all I'm saying."

Thomas spoke softly but in a clear and deliberate tone. "That kind of thinking could get her killed, you know that, don't you? Rupert Kly is not the sort of person to fool around with."

"I expect she knows better than anyone. That's what we're doing up here—making sure doesn't get killed."

Harley asked, "What's our first stop?"

"Lester and Gladys Nez's Place, see what we can learn there, then on up top to Rupert's camp."

"You don't think he's up there, do you?"

"No, but someone will be. Billy Red Clay says they run a good-sized band of sheep out of there, and a few cows too."

Even Thomas was surprised how rough and steep the road was going up to the camps. When they reached the Nez *hogan* they were amazed to see a canvas-top sheep wagon pulled up next to the dwelling. There was a team of mules in the pen behind it.

Harley indicated the sheepherder camp with a push of his chin. "Was that here the last time you came up, Charlie?"

"No, it wasn't."

Thomas shook his head. Well, one thing's for damn sure; they didn't bring that rig up the way we just came in."

Charlie agreed. "Billy Red Clay once said there was a back way into this place. One that connects to some old gas field roads. He says you can go all the way to Chaco Wash if you know what you're doing."

Thomas wondered out loud why they hadn't come in that way themselves?

Charlie was quick to answer. "I wanted to talk to Lester first, see if we can get some idea what's going on in the camps up on top. I don't want to walk into something we aren't prepared for up there."

Harley studied the set of mules a moment before reaching over to beep the horn. When he saw the team was okay with it, he waited another minute then did it again, but longer this time. The door opened a crack, and someone peeked out before turning back again. They could hear her saying something to someone before stepping outside. It was Gladys Nez buttoning up a light jacket as she stood outside the door. Shading her eyes with one hand, she could make out the Tribal emblem on the pickup and waited for someone to get out. The sun was well above the bluff now as it worked its way across a brilliant turquoise sky. Still, it was cold there in the shelter of the rim. Winter comes early to that country.

Charlie stepped down from the truck and held up a hand in greeting "*Yaa eh t'eeh*" he called, smiling. The woman looked at him a moment and turned back to the open door where she again spoke to someone inside. Finally recognizing the investigator, she came forward a few more steps, saying, "How are you, Mr. Yazzie? My husband was up all night with the sheep. He's just getting dressed but will be up and about in a minute or two."

Harley's eye went to the dead coyote hanging on the fence and knew the backstory of what she was saying.

Charlie shook his head, "Oh, I'm sorry to have to wake him up, tell him to take his time."

"No, it's alright, Mr. Yazzie. He was awake already; he was about to get up anyway. I've got some coffee on. You and your friends can come on in and have a cup. It'll take the chill off."

Charlie thanked the woman as he motioned to the two men in the truck to get down and come in. "It is pretty cool up here already, isn't it?" he asked her as the three men trooped in.

"Oh yes, the old people are saying it's going to be a cold one this winter." The woman ushered them in to the warmth of a pinyon wood fire which popped and crackled in a sheet-metal stove.

A baby's crib sat at the back of the room, and a man sat on the bed pulling on his boots. He looked up as the men entered, greeting them in old Navajo. Raking his fingers through his hair, Lester came to the table grinning. "How are you, Charlie? Good to see you again. I guess Gladys told you I been up all night with the sheep. The coyotes are so bad up here this year we had to split the band into two bunches to make it easier to watch them. It was my night to keep an eye on these closest to the place here. So, I didn't get much sleep."

Charlie nodded his understanding, then indicating the two men with him, said, "These are my friends Thomas Begay and Harley Ponyboy." The two men nodded to Lester and his wife...who bobbed her head without saying anything.

Harley asked, "Did they come in on you last night...the coyotes?"

"Only a few, I shot one and the others took off. They'll be back, though. They don't stay scared very long."

Having herded sheep as a boy, Harley knew what the man was talking about and clicked his tongue in sympathy. "No, they never stay gone very long, do they?"

Gladys brought cups and a pot of coffee, still at a rolling boil from the stove. She reached for a jug of cold water and dashed a small amount into the pot to settle the grounds. Pouring each cup nearly full, she made sure there was room left for canned milk and sugar. The men set to doctoring their coffee to their individual liking before taking long slurps from the still steaming cups.

Thomas nodded. "That's good coffee."

210

Gladys laughed. "It's this spring water we have up here. It's the best in this part of the country."

Lester agreed. "Everyone up on top comes down here for their drinking water. They say it's worth the haul."

Charlie looked toward the crib where some cooing could be heard. "How's that baby coming along? I don't remember hearing if it was a boy or a girl."

Gladys smiled and went to pick up the infant who made little noises as she brought her over into the light from the window so they might have a better look. "It's a girl baby."

Harley asked, "What is her name?" It was the polite thing to do.

Lester laughed, "She is only a few days old, so she doesn't have a name yet. Gladys' family believes in taking their time naming a child…they say that's the way it has always been done. They think you need to get some idea of who the baby is before giving them a name. I guess it sort of makes sense in a way. We'll come up with something in a day or two. In the meantime, we call her whatever comes to mind as we learn to get along with her."

Even though they had come on serious business, Charlie and the boys knew it would be rude to come to point of their visit too quickly and avoid the niceties.

The amenities were especially important to these more traditionally minded people here in the back country. It sometimes took them a little longer to warm up to strangers, though Lester and Gladys didn't seem to fall into that category.

After a little more chitchat it was Lester who finally asked, "How can we help you, Charlie? I know you boys didn't come all this way out here just to see our new baby."

The investigator chuckled. "I wish I could say that was why we came, Lester. But the truth is we need some help."

Gladys moved to the table to freshen their cups, saying, "You want to know where my father is, don't you, Mr. Yazzie?"

Charlie coughed quietly and cleared his throat. "I'm sorry, but yes, we desperately need to find him before someone else dies. There is no other way to put it."

Gladys shook her head. "No need for you to be sorry, Mr. Yazzie, I know what kind of man he is and what he has done over the years. You are right. All of us up here understand now that he has to be stopped and this is the time. This family has been afraid of him long enough."

Lester agreed. And in a quiet but emotional voice said, "Charlie, we will help in any way we can. We only learned of the death of Gladys's Aunt Glynda a day or so ago. It was her murder which finally made everyone realize something had to be done. Rosemary's death already had them thinking enough was enough." The young man hung his head and, with a deep sigh, said quietly, "Gladys told me a long time ago what happened with Billy Moon, back when she was young. She is willing to go to court against her father if it comes to that."

Charlie glanced over at Gladys who raised her head and nodded. "I heard him threaten my mother that day she went into town to talk to Billy Moon. Saying if she did, something bad would happen to her. We all knew he would do those things he threatened, too. But we're not afraid anymore, now that Billy Moon is back. We know she will stand up with us. It was what my father has always been afraid would happen." Tears were streaming down the young mother's face as Lester went to put his arm around her, comforting her as best he could.

Thomas and Harley seemed a little embarrassed, looking away and then back at Charlie, who appeared blindsided by this unexpected turn of events. It was more than he had hoped for. The investigator stood, indicating to Harley and Thomas the three would be waiting outside. Charlie was anxious to radio Billy Red Clay and let Agent Smith know what was going on, too.

Later, he advised both agencies of his intentions to continue their search for Rupert Kly. He told them he would also try to stay in contact with Arlene in his office, depending on the terrain and radio propagation.

Lester Nez soon came from the house assuring the three his wife was much better now and still firm in her conviction regarding her father. "Do you intend to go across the top and out that way?"

Charlie thought a moment. "It depends on what we learn from those people up there. We will stop and talk with them; someone must know something."

Lester nodded. "Gladys says Rupert's sister might be the one most likely to help. Rosemary's death changed her thinking on Rupert. Her name is Roberta John. Her husband David John died some years back, so she lives here with the family now. She is in fact, the head of the family now that Rupert is gone. She knows things about her brother no one else does. She may have some idea where he would be."

Charlie extended a hand. "Thanks, Lester, and thank Gladys for us, too. We'll keep you folks posted on what's going on. I'm sure it's uncomfortable not knowing where Rupert is or when he might show up. I can ask Billy Red Clay to send someone out here to keep an eye on the camps if you like?"

"Oh… No, Charlie, I think we'll be okay now that most of us are thinking alike." Lester had a determined look in his eye and appeared more than capable of taking care of his new family.

~~~~~~

The Kly camp consisted of several older *hogans,* built in the old way and surrounded by sheep corrals backed up to a crudely constructed lambing shed. A rock ridge rose to the north of the camp probably chosen to afford shelter from harsh spring winds during lambing. Some distance from the nearest dwelling, a couple of horses stood in a small pasture. Thomas thought the horses looked thin and ill-kept.

"Sheepherder horses all right," he said with a note of disdain. "Grass is about gone up here, and that stock pond to the east looks likely to go dry, too."

Harley Ponyboy surveyed the outfit with a more practiced eye. "Billy Red Clay told me these people ran a good-sized band up here. If they got their lambs off early enough last spring, they are maybe thinking about working a bunch back down-country about now. Winter's coming up here."

Thomas nudged him. "Only two trucks in the yard, and Rupert Kly's flatbed isn't one of them."

Charlie eased the Tribal unit up to the nearest *hogan*. And honked the horn. Almost instantly a woman opened the door, meaning she had been watching them come up the road—a thin, middle-aged woman, dressed in camp clothes that had seen better days. She inclined her head to one side, watching them a moment, and then boldly headed their way. The investigator rolled down the window but didn't get out of the truck—they were already running late.

"This must be Rupert's sister, Roberta John," he whispered.

The woman was nearly as tall as Thomas Begay and appeared quite sure of herself. She didn't invite them down but did offer her hand, which Charlie took and was surprised at the firm grip, unusual in a *Diné* woman.

"I expect you're looking for my brother Rupert. I'm Roberta John," she said. "One of our men noticed your truck down at the Nez place earlier this morning." She glanced down at the door's insignia, "Legal Services, I see. They told us a few days ago you had been down there about Rosemary. You must be Charlie Yazzie." She glanced through the window and apparently didn't recognize either of the other two men, so only nodded in their direction. Moving her gaze back to the investigator, she said in a low voice, "I guess you want to know where you can find Rupert?"

Charlie considered the woman a moment, she was both outspoken and educated, not what he expected. "You're his sister, is that right?"

"Yes, it is, though I hate to admit it anymore."

Charlie nodded, "I can understand that well enough Ms. John, but you are right. We do need to know where he is. No harm will come to him should he surrender peacefully. I can assure you he will receive fair treatment. Every law enforcement agency in the county is looking for him. This might be his last chance to offer himself up to his own people."

"To be honest with you, Mr. Yazzie, I am beyond caring what happens to him. He has shamed us and is considered '*Adáánii'* from now on. We will no longer speak his name among us, and he is not welcome in our camps. As far as his whereabouts goes, he has no real friends that I know of, only a few old cronies he used to hang out with. I do not know their names. And I do not want to know them. For us, Rupert Kly no longer exists." The woman turned and had taken several steps toward her home, when she turned suddenly and, as though it had just occurred to her, said, "When in town, he used to stay at a Farmington 'Indian bar'…they have rooms they rent, upstairs. I can't remember the name of the place, but it was run by a big rough looking Ute woman. Rupert pointed her out to me on the street one day. He said her name was Rosie. I haven't heard him mention that place in years...I don't know, it may not even be there anymore."

When they were well down the road Charlie asked softly, "So did everyone hear what the woman said about the bar in Farmington?"

Both men, looking straight ahead without the slightest expression, nodded their heads. After another mile Harley Ponyboy glanced sideways at Thomas Begay—the tiniest of smiles playing at the ends of his mouth. "Rosie's Place" he said with a sigh. "I haven't even driven by there in years...afraid to, I guess." He elbowed Thomas in the ribs. "Is it still there, would you know?"

"It was last month."

"Did you go in?"

"If you'll recall...Rosie and I had words, and she told me not to come back... Ever!"

"I do remember that. You, didn't pay her the four bucks you owed for your half the bar bill that night."

"Ahh, I did pay her back and with interest, too. It just took me a while getting around to it." Thomas smiled. "She still likes you though, Harley. Maybe you're the one who should drop in for a little chat with her. They still rent those rooms upstairs. I guess it's possible Rupert Kly still hangs out there. It's worth a shot, don't you think so, Charlie?"

The investigator gave the two a glance, saying, "Can't hurt, I suppose. He's got to be somewhere. I doubt the man will come back here, and he certainly won't go back to the *hogan* where Glynda Benally died. He'll be too superstitious to chance that. It seems he's running out of places to lay his head. Rosie Johnson's place is worth a look I suspect. We'll go back to town the long way; on the off chance we might run into someone out here who knows something."

Within less than two miles the three Navajo came up on a band of sheep apparently being moved down to winter pasture, just as Harley Ponyboy had predicted. The ewes still had the lambs on them. Which caused Harley to wonder if they were just taking the slower-moving bunch to better feed, waiting for the weather to move in before taking them all the way to the wintering grounds. That's where they would separate these larger market lambs.

Two older men were eating their lunch as they sat their horses and watched the band flow down-country. They didn't look at the three in the truck, just kept eating and following the sheep with their eyes.

Charlie eased the truck through the tail end of the ewes and sidled up next to the two riders. Rolling down the window he said hello in Navajo, and then asked the pair if they knew Rupert Kly.

One man had just taken a bite of his sandwich and chewed thoughtfully as he regarded the Legal Services shield on the pickup door. "I know him all right, but we haven't seen him for the last several days up here…coming or going. I heard there's a lot of law looking for him. I doubt you'll find him up here. I'd say he's already lit out for greener pastures."

"Any idea where that might be?"

"Albuquerque if he's smart. There's no one up here wants anything to do with him anymore. Myself, I'd keep on down to Old Mexico…if it was me."

Charlie nodded and rolled up the window. He doubted Rupert had ever been off the reservation. Unless he'd missed his guess, the man would not go so far as Mexico…or even Albuquerque. In Charlie's opinion Rupert would feel safer right here where he was born and grew up, rather than the big city where Billy Moon and her confederates might track him down. Here, the man knew the lay of the land, the few he could trust, and the many he couldn't. Rupert couldn't count on his family anymore, or his former friends, or those relatives in high places, they were all gone now. Dead, most of

them…or in jail. Still and yet, there would always people like him he could turn to—for a price.

That's what it would come down to, in the end,
digging those people out of their rat holes one at time.
Eventually, they'd find him.

12

The Chase

Back in town, Harley Ponyboy was duly elected to speak to Rosie Johnson regarding the murderous Rupert Kly. Charlie Yazzie would, obviously, get nowhere with the owner or her clientele, all of whom could spot a lawman from a great distance. As for Thomas Begay, he would have been their pick, if he hadn't been barred some years back. The big Ute bar owner was known for saying what she thought and for her long memory when it came to those deemed unwelcome in her establishment. The woman's word was law at the San Juan Social Club. The chances of Thomas being readmitted to that humble society were considered very unlikely.

Harley Ponyboy, on the other hand, was known to be a great favorite of the Ute woman. Not only because he paid his bar tab prior to leaving each night, but also, because Rosie Johnson just thought he was cute—cute being a rare quality among those known to frequent the place.

Charlie and Thomas dropped their friend off downtown in front of one of the few barber shops that catered to Indians—he didn't want to risk the chance someone might put the three of them together. It took Harley about twenty minutes to make his way to the establishment, what with the circuitous route he chose and stopping from time to time to gaze into store windows covertly watching for any who might follow.

He had been a soft touch for the down and outers during his drinking days, and now preferred not to excite their interest. He stood a moment just outside the establishment, which had remained surprisingly unchanged given the amount of time involved. The same lurid red neon over the door declared simply, "Cold Beer." The large lettering in the window still advertised "**The San Juan Social Club,**" though it had been newly repainted, somehow causing it to appear out of place. Down in one corner of the window was the small cardboard placard declaring: **Indians welcome.** This appeared to be the original fly-specked invitation—turning brown and curling around the edges.

It was mid-afternoon on a lazy Monday, and he couldn't imagine many patrons being inside at this early hour. The sound of the bell over the door sent a shiver of nostalgia through him. Dark and cool inside, the smell of stale beer and cigarette smoke hung over the interior like a veil. Seeing the same old picture over the bar still made him smile. An Indian Chief in full feather head-dress holding up a right hand in greeting. The caption was, "We have Reservations." Harley had spent many an hour sitting at the bar staring up at the old chief…going over in his mind what the many nuances of the words might intend, settling on a different version each time. Even then, it always brought a smile. Alongside the picture was yet another placard: "NO FIGHTING! OR YOUR ASS WILL BE OUT! This, along with a caricature of a braying donkey being pushed out the door. Each time he and Thomas Begay would come in, Rosie would raise a meaty fist and point to the sign in a threatening manner. Thomas Begay feared no man as far as Harley knew, still, he sometimes got the distinct impression the tall Navajo had come to dread Rosie Johnson.

There was only one or two older men scattered about the place. Sliding onto a bar stool, Harley watched as a man about his size came out of the back with a tray of fresh glasses. He was almost even with Harley when he, who was himself an Indian, sat the tray down and began arranging the glasses under the bar.

"What can I do you for, buddy?"

Harley smiled and held up a finger. "I'll just have a coke, with ice. I'm waiting for someone, and he hates it when I start drinking without him."

The man nodded with a grin and finished stacking the glasses before moving down to the soft drink dispenser, where he scooped up ice in a glass and began drawing the beverage, saying, "Name's Bob, by the way. I don't think I've seen you in here before, have I?"

"I'm Harley Ponyboy, I haven't been in for a while…you know how that goes." Looking toward the backroom he asked, "Does Rosie Johnson still run the place?"

"Oh yeah. She's just out doing some errands, should be back in a few. You know Rosie, do you?"

"I used to…but it's been a while since I've seen her. How's she doing these days?"

"Ah, mean as ever, I guess. Says she's going to sell out and move back to Towaoc…says the Ute are thinking about building a casino up there…but she's been saying that for a few years now. I'm from Towaoc, myself, born and raised." He frowned, "I guess that's why Rosie hired me…that, and I don't drink." He sighed, and there was a hint of worry in his voice when he said, "She's not in the best of health here lately. So, who knows, maybe she means it this time, about selling out…I mean." Bob took a swipe at the bar with a damp gray rag and lowered his voice. "I just don't know anymore, what she'll do."

The man was a talker, and in Harley's opinion, was the kind who made the best bartender. A person could sit home and drink, if he wanted to talk to himself. Harley had learned a lot about bartenders over the years. "Well, whatever it is with Rosie, I hope it's not anything too serious."

The bartender glanced at the front door as though he expected the woman might be standing there, listening. "I'm afraid it is serious."

The way Bob said it made Harley feel a little sad. He didn't ask any more about Rosie Johnson, instead changing the subject, he asked, "You wouldn't know a Rupert Kly, would you, Bob?"

The barman put down the glass he was polishing, cocking his head a little as if considering the question. "He's not who you're waiting for, is he?"

"No, not hardly. A friend of mine is looking for him that's all, I told him I'd ask around."

"I didn't think you looked the type to hang with someone like that."

"So, you do know him?"

"I know *of* him, and that's all I care to know. He eyed Harley a moment longer. "Rosie barred Rupert

226

some time back." Bob frowned. "Your friend, you're waiting for, he isn't a lawman, is he?"

"Not really, he's a lawyer. A client of his is looking for Kly, a family member I guess."

"Harley," he said with a grin, "I'm sure you remember Rosie don't like cops of any kind…and she doesn't like the help passing out information about her patrons, either."

"I know her well enough, Bob, well enough to know Rupert's not the sort she would try to protect."

Bob grinned. "No. I guess he's not at that, and since he's barred, I guess he's no longer a customer either." He glanced again at the door and leaning into the bar, lowered his voice to a whisper. "Rupert came in here, night before last, and wanted a room upstairs. Rosie told him he wasn't welcome here and he'd better hit the road. He started giving her some lip—I hadn't come on shift yet, myself—but later, a couple of regulars who were sitting there at the bar, told me what happened."

Bob licked his upper lip as if he were visualizing the encounter. "This Rupert fella reached across the bar and grabbed Rosie by the wrist. Rosie's a big woman, Harley, and has a God-awful reach on her. And this was the kind of thing she considers part of the job. She knows what she's doing when it comes to handling a drunk who gets out of line. She opened that big fist of hers and, latching onto Rupert's wrist, reared back, pulling him partway across the bar. And that's when she clobbered him upside the head with a heavy right. They said you could have heard it out in the street." Bob hesitated a moment and took a deep breath.

By now, Harley's left eye was twitching, his own hands silently clenching and unclenching as he envisioned the struggle. He'd seen the woman in action a time or two over the years and had personally witnessed the mayhem those big fists could wreak. He fidgeted as Bob paused for effect. "Well, what'd she do then, Bob?"

"They said she grabbed the man by the hair and smacked his face into the bar...right about where you're sitting now, Harley. Not just once, but twice, quicker than an eye could follow. That's how they put it. They said Rupert sort of pushed himself up off the bar and began backing up 'til he hit a table, and then just turned and stumbled out the door."

Harley couldn't believe his ears. "Well, that's just the damndest thing I've ever heard."

"Me too, Harley, me too... I've seen some fights in here, but nothing like this...it wasn't a fight really, it was more like a massacre. I came in to take my shift just after Rupert left. Rosie was still behind the bar wiping up blood with a bar rag. I could see there'd been a

228

hell'uva confrontation of some sort and asked her, was she all right."

Bob coughed and cleared his throat. "She nodded her head yes, saying, 'If that son-of-a-bitch ever comes back in here, Bob, I'm gonna kill him!" The barman gazed out across the dimly lit room with a scowl. "I grew up around the woman up at Towaoc and Cortez…she'll kill him sure as hell, if he comes back." He picked up his own bar rag and wiped down the bar again as though he couldn't get it clean enough.

Harley nodded and getting down from his stool, said, "Bob, it's been a pleasure talking to you. I don't think there's any use in me waiting any longer for my friend…he must have stopped in some other watering hole. I have to be moving along myself now, Bob…before my wife takes it into her head to come looking for me."

The bartender smiled as he raised a hand in farewell, watching as the little man headed for the door. Bob thought it unfortunate that Rosie Johnson had missed her old friend, thinking it might have made her feel better. The barman wished more of their patrons could be as pleasant as this good-natured Harley Ponyboy.

Just outside the door, Harley was stopped by a man he had seen leaving the bar ahead of him. An older, poorly dressed man who clearly had been whiling away the afternoon drinking and waiting for someone he could put the arm on.

"Say fella, you couldn't spare a man a dollar, could you?"

Harley was about to step around him, when he recognized him from some years back. "Is that you Johnny?"

The man only nodded. "I heard you asking about Rupert Kly in there, but I thought I'd wait to make sure it was you, Harley."

Harley looked up and down the street before asking, "Do you know where he might be, Johnny? I'm looking for the man and would appreciate any help I can get." So, saying, he reached in his pocket and pulled out five one-dollar bills, holding them out for the man to see.

Johnny first held up a hand, as though the money wasn't necessary, but Harley kept the bills out there. And when he saw the man lick his lips—like a horse when he's finally willing to cooperate—Harley nodded and again urged the bills on him.

This time the man took the money and stuffed it in his pocket. He then assured Harley, the man he was looking for was out at the homeless camp under the bridge across the San Juan. At least he had been there when he'd left for town that afternoon. "He's camped down in the willows in that little bunch of cottonwoods, if you know where I mean?"

Harley smiled. He knew exactly where it was and said, "You take care of yourself, Johnny," and turned to go.

He was only a few steps away when the man called to him, "He has a rifle in that flat-bed truck, Harley."

Harley didn't turn, or slow down, but raised a hand in acknowledgment. He'd spotted Charlie and Thomas pulling over to the curb halfway up the block and hurried to join them. It was coming on twilight and the streets lights were beginning to flicker on. It was warmer down here in town, and the wind had died down making for a pleasant walk. He hoped Charlie and Thomas would decide not to move on the homeless camp until morning...but knew this wasn't likely.

Thomas opened the door and stepped down to let Harley in the middle so everyone would be more comfortable. The three men sat there a minute in silence.

Thomas sniffed a couple of times. "You reek of smoke and alcohol, Harley." He turned and took a deep breath. "It smells good. How was Rosie?"

"She's dying, Thomas, according to the bartender." He sighed audibly. "I didn't see her myself. I

231

didn't really want to see her after hearing how bad off she was."

Thomas took on a sorrowful expression. "I didn't think anything could kill that woman."

"She was still strong enough to knock the crap out of Rupert yesterday."

All three men smiled at this. Thomas said in a small voice, "I would like to have seen that."

"Oh, they said it was something, alright. Rosie apparently smacked the hell out of him, beat his head against the damn bar."

Charlie cleared his throat. "Anyone happen to mention *where* she ran him off *to*, Harley?"

"No, but outside the bar, 'Johnny the Mooch' told me Kly's out at the homeless camp by the river."

Thomas seemed irate, "We've been running all over hell and back, looking for the bastard, and there he is all snugged in, right down there next to town?"

"That's what Johnny said. He also said Rupert had a rifle with him."

Charlie smiled. "We pretty much guessed that didn't we, Harley?"

Harley grinned. "Yes, but it's always nice to have an eyewitness who can take the guesswork out of it, huh?"

The investigator turned the key in the ignition and, putting the Chevy in gear, started to pull away from the curb. The screech of brakes had him instantly twisting the wheel back into the curb. The siren on the sheriff's patrol car yelped as it whipped in front of them. The deputy on the passenger side smiled as he lifted a finger and waggled it a time or two, grinning at the three in the Tribal police unit.

Charlie rolled down the window but didn't recognize the deputy. *Doesn't matter,* he thought, he knew who was driving.

Sheriff Dud Schott extended a hand up where they could see it and motioned for them to follow him. At the nearby sheriff's office, Dud pulled into his allocated space and directed the Tribal unit to take the slot next to him. On the way there, none of the three men in the pickup had said a single word to each other. The sheriff got out of the car and came around to Charlie's window with rather a grim expression on his face.

"Good evening, gentlemen. You boys have had a very busy day, haven't you?"

Harley and Thomas glanced at each other but didn't say anything. They knew enough to let Charlie do the talking. All three men had a long and unhappy history with the county lawman.

The tribal investigator looked the sheriff up and down, before speaking. "Dud, what can we do for you? We were just on our way home to supper. I expect you know how that is, you being a married man, and all."

"Ahh, yes, Charlie, I do know how that is." There was an edge to the sheriff's voice they were all too familiar with. "I haven't even had my lunch yet, for following you boys around since you hit town this afternoon."

Charlie frowned as he glanced at his companions. They frowned back, shrugging their shoulders in lieu of a reply.

"Would you like a sandwich, Dud? I think we've got one left over from lunch."

The lawman slowly shook his head.

"How did you know where to find us, Dud?"

"It wasn't too hard, Charlie. And, in this case, I don't mind telling you. I called your house. Your daughter was the only one home, and I have to say I have never talked to a more honest and forthright young lady. She told me where you and these other two old-timers were off to this morning. I put out a bulletin on your truck and you were spotted coming back into town this afternoon. You three splitting up, I admit, made things a little tougher. We almost lost Harley at one point, but I knew if we kept tagging along after you, he'd turn up." Dud's tone changed, becoming even brighter as he went on. He was on the verge of laughing when he said, "Oh, and by the way, two of my undercover officers have had Rupert Kly under surveillance for hours."

"Did Sasha tell you where *he* was, too?"

"No, Charlie, Johnny the Mooch called our office, saying he'd heard there was a reward out for the man and thought he knew where we could find him. Simple as that. He also told us the three of you were on his trail."

Harley leaned out around Charlie and innocently asked, "Dud, do you mind if I inquire how much the reward is?"

The sheriff chuckled. "Not at all, Harley, we posted it this morning. If Charlie had checked in with anyone today, he'd have heard about it. Now everyone in town knows. It's five thousand dollars."

Harley looked at Thomas, and Thomas looked at Harley. Both men beamed as though pleased to hear it.

Charlie Yazzie finally asked the question he was really wondering about. "Dud, it seems you have this thing all tied up. Why is it you haven't moved in on him before now?"

"Well, that's the beauty of it, boys. It's to avoid him getting away, you know, like he got away from you and Billy Red Clay up at his camp in the Chuskas." Dud grinned, smug in the knowledge a reckoning in their long era of animosity was close at hand. "We've called in every spare law enforcement officer in San Juan County. As we speak, a cordon is being drawn around that entire camp there on the river. I doubt a ground-squirrel could get past that line. I just wanted to warn you boys not to show up down there and cause any un-due confusion." Dud looked past Charlie and directly at Harley Ponyboy. "This may be Johnny the Mooch's lucky day, Harley, I mean in addition to those five dollars he got off you."

Thomas nudged Harley Ponyboy and whispered something. Charlie cocked his head to hear but couldn't quite make it out.

Harley, looking out of the window nodded his head and smiled at his lanky companion. He tapped Charlie on the shoulder and whispered, "Thomas thinks it's about time to go."

Charlie Yazzie said, "Dud, we appreciate you bringing us up to date on all this. It's gratifying to see our agencies are finally beginning to work together for the common good. However, we really do have to get along home. You be sure and give me a call when you have the man in custody. It will be a weight off my mind knowing he's locked up." Charlie backed the truck up as Dud Schott registered a momentary look of doubt as he waved them off.

Thomas turned and looked across Harley Ponyboy at the investigator. "What the hell was that all about? How did Dud Schott get mixed up in this?"

Charlie grimaced. "Well, he is the sheriff of this county. You'll notice he didn't make his move until we were off the reservation and back in his jurisdiction. I'm not going to say he's getting any smarter, but he's certainly better informed. The information my daughter supplied and what Johnny the Mooch must have told them, might have explained some of it. But there's still a few questions I would like to have answered." He picked up the mic, and when Arlene came on, asked her to have him patched through to Agent Fred Smith's office. In only a few minutes, the radio buzzed, and Charlie picked up.

"Yes, Investigator Yazzie, this is Agent Smith's secretary. You just caught me going out the door. Fortunately, I was working a little late this evening. How can I help you?"

Charlie glanced at his watch and frowned. "I don't suppose Fred is still in, is he?"

"No, sir, Agent Smith is out on assignment and currently out of our coverage area. He did, however, call in earlier to see if you had checked in. I have tried to reach him several times in the last couple of hours with no luck. He did say earlier he would be back before dark, so I expect he's on his way in and should be back in town shortly. I can leave a message for him to call you as soon as he arrives, if that's all right, Investigator?"

"Yes, Frances, I suppose that will have to do, thank you." Hanging the mic back on the dash clip Charlie turned to the others. "Well, she said she would leave him a message. So, I guess we'll just have to wait until he calls us."

Thomas Begay turned to the side window and gazed into the gathering darkness. "I wonder where Billy Red Clay is?"

Staring straight ahead, Charlie flipped on the headlights. "Well, I'm pretty sure he's off duty now, and if I were to guess, I would say your nephew is probably somewhere very close to the RV park and Billy Moon's bus. He will be keeping an eye on her and her daughter, whether they know it or not."

Harley spoke in a quiet voice, "You don't suppose Rupert Kly knows where those two women are, do you?" Then raising an eyebrow said, "That RV park is only a mile or so from the river bridge, and their bus is pretty easy to spot."

Thomas Begay nodded. "That may be what he was doing there to start with. What better place to hide out than right under their noses?"

Thomas frowned. "I hope my nephew knows what's going on, and not letting that girl get in the way of his thinking."

13

The Fugitive

Rupert Kly was accustomed to staying one step ahead of the law and over the years had become quite good at it. His old pickup truck was on its last legs and had, in fact, been lucky to make it as far as the homeless camp. There was nothing incriminating left in the truck, he was too smart for that, his rifle now at the bottom of the muddy San Juan.

When he'd first learned who Billy Moon had become, he was appalled. Certain she would one day return or send someone after him. Once again, he had anticipated what the woman was capable of.

For years he had dreaded this day but now that it had come, felt relieved. Already her main protector was seriously injured and in the hospital. It was, of course, on him that the man was still alive at all. Any ordinary person would have died in his tracks. He still could take care of that though, just as he had Rosemary and Glynda. Both women had known too much and had already spilled their guts to Billy Moon. Most likely one of them had been on the verge of talking to the law, as well. Two down and two still on his 'to do' list.

Oh, I had nearly forgotten Wayne Moon, the girl's father, but that had been so long ago it probably wouldn't matter anymore. Not to me it doesn't. Rupert smiled to himself at the recollection of Wayne pleading for his life, saying there would be no one to take care of his daughter. Well, he took care of Billy Moon himself and, with any luck at all would continue to take care of her—but permanently this time. No one could say he hadn't been a good father to his own daughters including Irene, the youngest.

These things, of course were not the full extent of the evil deeds he had done. No, not at all. His relatives in high places had needed a little work done from time to time, and he had been glad to help them out. To his mind it had been good insurance, and they in turn would go the distance for him when a little behind the scenes protection was needed…or else. *All those people are gone now,* Rupert reflected, *leaving me alone here to fend for myself.* Yet even with this latest crisis, he still reckoned he had some good years left—if he remained cautious and had a little luck. That had been his nickname when younger—Lucky Kly, he was called by those who knew and feared him most. *No reason I can't weather this little storm jut as I have all the others.*

When he had talked to Johnny the Mooch earlier, he boasted of the reward that was out on him, knowing full well the man would soon figure out how easy it would be to make his fortune. It would be too great a temptation for the weak little man to resist.

Before he left that afternoon, Rupert poured what little gas he could drain from his truck's tank over the interior of the flatbed, then lit it on fire. As the towering plume of smoke was seen from the top of hill, it was only moments before the wail of sirens could be heard heading that direction. And by the time a crowd gathered, the fire engines were there and going into action. Rupert Kly was already well on his way.

~~~~~~

The sheriff's deputies were on the scene but standing back and forming a cordon around the entire camp and beyond. First, deputies thought Rupert was still in the truck, but that could not be ascertained until the vehicle cooled enough for someone to make certain. A camp resident had come forward to say he thought he saw Rupert asleep in the truck. When the deputies took a closer look, it was obvious the fugitive wasn't in the vehicle. Still, after consulting with his spotters at the top of the hill, who said they'd seen no one leave the camp—Dud was convinced the man remained within that considerable area of cottonwoods and brush deputies had cordoned off. The sheriff was adamant his deputies should tighten the noose until they found the fugitive. It was an election year, and Dud needed to turn the increasingly negative tide pounding his poll numbers. Apprehending a high-profile serial killer might be just the ticket, to Dud's way of thinking.

~~~~~~~

Charlie pulled his unit into the parking area at the top of hill, and the three men inside sat silently surveying the mass of law enforcement cars and personnel encircling the area alongside the river. As the cordon tightened around the homeless camp, various residents were seen attempting a last-minute escape. One old lady was so incensed when deputies told her to leave, she confronted the advancing lawmen…with rude gestures and a barrage of verbal abuse. Though she could not be heard distinctly, her intent was clear enough. Waving her arms and stomping her feet, she made for the nearest officers, threatening them with what appeared to be a stick or cane of some sort. An old man chased after her, seemingly to dissuade the woman from continuing her rampage, but without any apparent effect.

Harley Ponyboy nudged Thomas Begay and pointed at a Tribal police unit turning in. "Here comes your nephew…"

Both Charlie and Thomas turned at the same time, giving the young policeman's freshly washed vehicle the eye.

"Still trying to impress Irene, I see." Charlie reckoned. I doubt he's been gone long."

Thomas chortled. "More like trying to impress her mother…if he's smart as he thinks he is. Billy Moon will have the final say in the end, I expect."

"Maybe…" Charlie murmured under his breath, not fully convinced either woman could sway the other when it came to matters of the heart. From what he'd seen, the mother and daughter were so alike it would be difficult to say who might prevail—strong women, each in her own way.

Charlie turned to the Tribal officer as he came rushing up, red-faced and out of breath. But before Billy Red Clay could say anything, the investigator asked calmly, "You didn't happen to see anything of Rupert Kly down there, did you?"

"Hell, yes, I saw him. Fred Smith had already called me to say one of his informants *thought* he saw Kly talking to Johnny the Mooch down there at the homeless camp. I thought from the beginning the man would be hanging out somewhere around here. That's why I've been staying close by, keeping watch on the women's tour bus. Just before the fire started, I walked over here with my binoculars. I had already spotted Rupert's old flatbed down there the night before but couldn't see any sign of him around it." Billy shook his head and grimaced. "I was up all night, anyway, so walked over here a time or two to have a look at the camp. It was too dark to see much, so I stayed close to the bus the rest of the night. But I made it a point to be up here at first light this morning and sure enough, after only a few minutes, Rupert comes crawling out of the brush and stood looking at his truck a minute or two and then turned back the way he had come. Apparently, he made a nest for himself out there in the brush and was out of sight…hunkered down. Later that afternoon, as I made my rounds, I stopped to study the truck for several minutes—and eventually, an arm reached out from under it and pulled a cooking pot back under there. I couldn't figure out what anyone would be doing under that truck with a cooking pot."

When Billy finally stopped to catch his breath, the three listeners stood speechless, slack-jawed and staring. Finally, his Uncle Thomas spoke up, "Did it ever occur to you to call in and report Rupert was down there?"

"Hell, Uncle, the sheriff's crew was all over the place by then but keeping out of sight for the most part. They obviously knew the man was down there, or they wouldn't have been sneaking around to form a cordon."

It was then that Charlie held up a hand to tone things down a notch. "Just go on with your story, Billy, so we can try to piece this business together and see where we're at."

The policeman stopped a moment as if to gather his thoughts. "It wasn't much later, that even more cops began filtering in to re-form the cordon around the camp. Maybe, that's what they had been waiting for…more cops to make a tighter cordon. I couldn't tell for sure what they were doing from up here." He glance around and shifted from foot to foot. There seemed to be a lot of confusion. But it was only a few minutes later Rupert crawled out from under his truck with the pot and throwing it through the open window, tossed a match in after it. When the truck burst into flames, he ran back into the brush. There was a good breeze blowing down off the hill at the time which pushed the fire toward the cordon, scattering lawmen every which way as they ran from the flames. The fire department can't be more than a half-mile from here and they were enroute, sirens blaring—within seconds it dawned on me what his plan was. I then concentrated my glasses on the north-west side of the camp next to the river, figuring that's where Kly would come out. Several other camp people did come out that way."

Harley Ponyboy shook his head, disgust written on his face. "He didn't come out, did he?"

Billy scowled and shaking his head at the little man went on with his story. "The law was still scattered around the south end of the area but beginning to re-group. It looked to me like some of them must have thought Kly might still be in the vehicle—you know, died in the fire. After things cooled down it must have been obvious there was no one in the cab."

"So, he got away again, did he?" Thomas turned and spit in the dust as his nephew looked away.

"The man has more guts than a government mule." Billy declared. "Anyone who would lay out there in the brush all day with cops running back and forth everywhere, has got to be stone-cold crazy…or just doesn't give a damn."

Thomas, as if not willing to let it go, said, "Billy, I think we've already agreed the man is crazy. The question is, where will he turn up next?"

Harley jumped in again. "Ha, I wouldn't be surprised if he was hiding within earshot of us right now!"

The others flinched at that, casting suspicious glances toward the hedges and small clumps of trees the city recently planted nearby. Already a few of the campers, now truly homeless, and bereft of even their previous poor accommodations, began straggling past on their way downtown and possibly to some liquid refreshment. Several paused to scope out the city's little landscaping project as a possible temporary substitute for the night's lodgings.

Charlie watched as a local patrolman stopped to admonish the people not to stop this close to the hospital or downtown area. The city would set up a designated shelter, he said, but didn't say when that might happen or where. It was about this time the old lady with the cane and her husband labored up the hill, faces smudged and eyes red from the smoke. She immediately barged through the bystanders and in a loud voice began berating the officer as she had the lawmen down below. "When the wind shifted," she said, "and the fire turned back on our camp, I heard the sheriff tell the firemen to

248

'just let it burn.' That's how they treat us old Inyan' people these days."

The patrolman, holding up a cautionary finger, went on in as kind and considerate a way possible under the circumstances, again assuring all that would listen they would be offered shelter in a timely manner.

The old woman, muttering to herself that there would be no help for them here, sought out her husband and the two hobbled after the others who were already some distance ahead.

Charlie was quite aware the homeless had been a thorn in the sheriff's side for the past several years. The camp, however, was on land some thought to be still under Tribal jurisdiction, thus efforts to remove the people had come to a legal standoff. Cleaning the place out had been on Dud's campaign agenda for some time now, and the man had come to believe he had the support of many of his constituents. Though Rupert Kly had evaded him this time the sheriff did, at least, have the consolation of fulfilling this particular campaign promise.

The three men followed the ongoing confrontation a minute or two longer and then finally turned away.

"Half those people will be in jail tonight," Thomas noted sadly, as if contemplating their almost certain fate. There had been a time when he himself had been headed for such an end. And if it hadn't been for

Lucy Tallwoman, it might well have been him standing there looking at another night in jail.

Billy Red Clay, who had also been watching, threw up his hands in frustration, saying. "None of us even knows what Kly looks like for sure. I've only seen him at a distance myself. The man could be standing right over there with those people, and we wouldn't know it." Billy shook his head. "I'm not doing any good here. I'd better get back over to the RV park and make sure Irene and her mother are alright."

Thomas nodded, "One thing for sure, those women *do* know what he looks like and are now on their guard. I don't think he'll try anything this soon…but I guess you never know what a guy like this will try, do you?" Then turning to Harley, he chuckled. "I imagine Johnny the Mooch might have to wait a while longer for his reward, wouldn't you say?"

His friend snorted, "I think this has turned into a new ballgame alright—that reward is probably already up for grabs again."

Charlie, raising his eyebrows at this, addressed the policeman, saying, "I think you're right, Billy. It's probably best you stay close over there at the bus until we hear something. Harley, Thomas, and I will be in the area for a while until things settle down and may poke around on our own. Who knows, maybe we'll get lucky."

The three men stood talking a moment as they watched Billy pull out of the overlook.

Rethinking a moment, the investigator's new thought was that they drop by Billy Moon's tour bus themselves, not only to assure the women they would be in the area, but to gauge Billy Moon's state of mind. On their arrival, however, they were surprised to see Federal Agent Fred Smith just getting out of his government car with a sheaf of papers in hand.

Charlie pulled in alongside the FBI man's vehicle and rolled down his window. The two next to him exchanged glances and focused their attention on an inspection of the headliner. Fred came around to Charlie's window.

"Well, boys, I see you made it back to town alright."

The Legal Services inspector nodded and mumbled something about coming back in the long way. Clearing his throat, he went on. "Fred, I guess you've already heard about the sheriff's failed plan down at the homeless camp?"

The hint of a grim smile passed between the two as they looked in that direction. Occasional whisps of smoke still could be seen drifting up from the ashes below the brow of the hill. As they spoke, the big fire engines could be heard laboring up the hill. The chief declared the emergency over but left a mop up crew on duty for the remainder of the day…just to make sure.

Fred refocused his attention on the investigator, "Yes, yes, I did hear that. I was even able to catch some of it on my scanner on the way into town. Later, one of my spotters stationed there on the overlook, filled me in." Fred shook his head as if in amazement, "It's a wonder no one was killed down there. Billy Red Clay confirmed the report only moments later, saying Rupert Kly, was likely on the run again."

"I would have to agree with that, Fred. We'll get him, though, that's for certain. The fact is he has no place to go."

Fred, as usual, appeared neither pleased nor displeased as he said, "Billy mentioned you boys were a little late to the party out here. But said you had been delayed by the Sheriff temporarily taking you into custody. What, for God sakes, was that all about?"

Charlie coughed as though something had momentarily become stuck in his craw. "Oh, nothing really, Fred…you know Dudley, never misses a chance to exert his self-proclaimed authority. He didn't really take us into custody but went to great lengths to make clear how he intended to catch the notorious Rupert Kly. Went so far as to warn us not to meddle in the operation, which he declared was already well in progress. He himself would, he said, be marshaling his incoming troops from a closer proximity to his communication tower. Said reception was poor down on the river."

Fred sighed heavily and rolled his eyes. "Yes, well, we've now seen how well that worked out for him, haven't we? The sheriff's going to have a lot to answer for this election year. And I'm thinking this latest little ill-advised effort may have been his swan song." Smiling wanly, the senior agent raised his sheaf of papers and declared, "This is what I'm here for. I've been in Albuquerque all day going over these autopsy reports, rushed through by the director himself. He wanted me to be down there personally for his explanation of the forensics involved. Not just for Rupert Kly's two wives but for the long-delayed evaluation of what is now known regarding the death of Billy Moon's father, which in my own view might be the last word on the subject. The case file will remain open, of course, but unless something new surfaces, this is it." Seeing the warning shift in Charlie's glance, the agent turned to see Billy Moon and her daughter standing unannounced behind him. Smoothly shifting gears without the slightest trace of surprise, he said quietly, "I'm sorry you ladies had to hear that. I had hoped to leave this information with you in private…which I will do if we can go inside."

Billy Moon nodded, and motioned for Charlie, to accompany them inside, as if knowing she might have need of his legal expertise. Her daughter Irene, opted to stay outside, as did Harley and Thomas. The younger woman glanced down the street at Officer Red Clay's Tribal unit and waved while beckoning him to join them.

Inside the tour bus and comfortably seated, the FBI man spread the papers on the table. All had been properly correlated as to each individual case. Billy Moon brought a decanter of cold water and glasses from the galley, which she filled and passed out without comment.

Fred thanked her and took a sip before removing a photo from the inside pocket of his jacket. "Billy, I would appreciate you having a look at this photo of Rupert Kly. It's from local police files from years back but hopefully represents a reasonable likeness yet today."

Billy, looking suddenly older, took the photo and with a nearly imperceptible shudder, grimly focused on the likeness. Nodding her head without speaking she handed the image back. Then taking a moment to compose herself, said, "That is Rupert Kly as I remember him."

Fred passed the item to Charlie, saying, "This is a copy for your own file. I will see that Tribal police gets a copy as well." He looked across at Billy Moon. "Now for the autopsy reports…if you still feel up to it, Billy?"

The woman took a deep breath and nodded to indicate her willingness to proceed.

Fred then looked at Charlie, saying, "Should you have any question or prefer Billy not answer any specific question I might have, please feel free to speak up, Charlie. I will leave copies of everything with you, and you may give access to your client, should she request it. I see no need to show photos of the murder victims at this time, however, they will be included in the reports I leave with you. I will also couch the medical terminology in plain English as much as I'm able. Just as the Bureau director in Albuquerque explained it to me." Taking another sip of water, Fred took up the first set of papers. "In the case of Glynda Benally, the woman was shot inside her own residence and at close range by a person or persons unknown. She died almost instantly as far as could be told, by a single shot to the head from a high-powered rifle. One fired from approximately seventy-five yards away. Our forensic people found the entire crime scene straightforward and consistent with the visible evidence. The killer was apparently waiting for the woman when she arrived home from town. There was no sign of a struggle or other confrontation, the shot being fired through the open door." Fred looked up, as though to see how well Billy was taking this information.

Without any facial expression, Billy nodded that he should continue.

Fred made a note or two in the margin of the report before going on. "It was determined that the later intrusion of the wounded Tito Alvarez occurred some hours after the Benally woman died. Alvarez has so far, been unable, or unwilling, to give his version of the discovery of the remains. Two additional spent shell casings were recovered by our forensics people from another site only a short distance away from the first." Fred paused a moment for yet another drink of water and then went on. "It was later ascertained by Legal Services Tracker Harley Ponyboy that Alvarez was shot as he approached the *hogan*, taking a total of two shots to the body. Three spent cartridges were found some distance from the victim, indicating the shooter may have missed with at least one shot and possibly two, assuming there was a spent shell casing carried away in his rifle. Despite being grievously injured, Alvarez was able to make his way back to the road and his vehicle, before collapsing—later to be discovered by Tribal Investigator Charlie Yazzie and his assistants, one of whom, called in Search and Rescue, who in turn transported Alvarez to the local Farmington hospital."

Charlie glanced at Billy Moon, her expression stoic. She had started this mess when she came back to town, but for her, it began when Rupert Kly first abused her. He couldn't hold it against the woman for wanting revenge. But at what cost?

Fred picked up his glass of water, swirled the little remaining, took a sip and then set the glass back down. "The remains of Glynda Benally were recovered the next morning by a ground team sent by our office. While this concludes the information we have on the Benally woman, we hasten to add the fact that we still do not have conclusive evidence of who the person was who fired the fatal shots. There is a fugitive still at large that we strongly suspect of the crime, but until Mr. Alvarez can tell us what he knows, we are unable to make a final determination of guilt in the murder. In the meantime, we are continuing to monitor the wounded man's condition and will, hopefully, soon have some corroborative evidence of what the witness saw out there."

At this time both men looked to Billy Moon, obviously hoping she might at last offer up what she had admitted was some sort of undisclosed information she'd learned from Tito not long after he was brought

257

into the hospital. "Billy, are you sure you don't want to tell us what Tito said to you in the intensive care unit?"

The woman only sighed, staring back at the two men as though she didn't know what they were talking about.

Looking down at the floor with what appeared to be a sad expression, the FBI agent picked up the second file and began to speak. "In the case of Rosemary Kly...first wife of Rupert Kly...the coroner has determined neighbors found the woman dead alongside a rural road not far from her home. When the body was discovered, it was taken to the home she shared with her daughter and son-in-law." And though it was some hours before the remains could be recovered, the medical examiner was able to offer us a few things we weren't aware of in our cursory examination at her home. Her left ankle was only fractured and not actually broken, as I had first thought in my initial investigation. The doctor further theorized, this most likely led to the fall that precipitated the more serious break in the hip. It is conceivable the ensuing fall also caused the head injury that led to her eventual death." Fred looked up at the woman. "Billy, please keep in mind, I am only paraphrasing the more technical medical jargon in this report—which will be made available to you for a more in-depth opinion of the report."

Billy nodded her understanding and again motioned the agent to continue.

"Due to the fact that the original death scene had been compromised by the removal of the body— before the FBI Forensics team had a chance to make their examination—we can only presume, at this point, what really took place up in the Chuskas that night." Fred paused and rechecked his notes, "What the coroner is saying in his final summation, is that his investigation shows no real evidence the death was due to criminal intent, or, in other words, it might well have been an accident. Even the previous threats and warnings Rupert Kly made against his wife would not likely decide a jury. Without an eyewitness account, or an outright confession, Rupert Kly would probably walk out of that courtroom a free man—regardless of what we *think* we know. Again, the same thing can be said of the Benally death. Without the testimony of Tito Alvarez in *this* case, the outcome would be in grave doubt."

Billy Moon appeared stunned, nearly speechless as she came to understand the lack of real evidence in the case. She turned to her investigator, "Is this how you see things playing out at trial, Charlie?"

Charlie pursed his lips in thought for a moment. Then sighing, nodded, "I'm afraid so, Billy. I'm sure Fred and his people are already running down leads in both cases. But so far, in either case, there is nothing to tie Rupert to the death of the woman beyond a handful of shell casings. There is no murder weapon, and at this point, I seriously doubt there ever will be one. Now, everything hinges on Tito and what he might have to offer in lieu of our rather weak suppositions."

The three of them sat quietly for a moment as the reality of the situation sank in for Billy. "And what of my Father's case?" she asked, "Is it the same thing there? Is there nothing beyond the little we already knew?"

Fred tapped the last report with a finger but could only shake his head in reply. "Sadly, Billy, no other determination could be made beyond what's already known. Without a previously unknown witness coming forward...or the unlikely event of a confession of guilt...this will have to go into the cold case files in hope some future new technology might shed more light on his death."

Billy seemed to go limp for an instant, as though life itself had flown from her, leaving only a shell of her iron-will holding her up. Her expression changed before their eyes, leaving something hard and unfathomable Charlie could not define.

Clearly alarmed, the investigator reached to touch her hand, only to have her recoil and look away.

She gazed past them and through the screened door of the bus. "So, this is the way it all ends, is it?" Then remarked quietly, "Tito said as much when I spoke with him at the hospital. He told me he hadn't been able to make out who it was shooting at him. The person stayed hidden in the underbrush, he said." Billy smiled crookedly as she said, "I'm sure he would have lied for me if I had asked, but I couldn't bring myself to do that. He also knew there was something wrong with him, inside, he said. He had known it for a long time. That's why he wanted to take care of Rupert, while he was still able to do it."

The two men exchanged glances. Charlie, nodded to her. "That's the reason you didn't want to tell us what he said, isn't it?"

Billy Moon didn't look at them and remained silent as she avoided their questioning gaze.

~~~~~~~

As the two lawmen walked back out to their vehicles, neither was happy with the information they had come away with. Fred had hoped Billy would divulge more regarding her last conversation with Alvarez. Information pointing a finger at Rupert Kly, implicating him as Glynda Benally's killer and verifying his attempt to murder Tito as well. That would have afforded them an iron-clad case against the man, sufficient to put him away with a life sentence, at the least.

For his part, Charlie Yazzie felt guilty, thinking he might have lulled Billy into a false sense of believing Rupert was as good as convicted, only to have her disappointed at the last minute. The FBI would maintain the ongoing investigation of the deaths of the two women of that, he was sure. Not to mention the attempted murder of Alvarez. Fred was not one to be easily discouraged, nor was he for that matter.

The FBI agent stopped at his car door and turned to the Legal Services investigator. "You know, Charlie, this isn't the end of it. We do have a witness to Rupert setting the fire, which endangered lives and destroyed property. Officer Red Clay saw it all and will attest to it in court. Arson is a serious charge and, when apprehended, will keep the man in jail for some time. Sufficient time hopefully, to allow us to find further evidence of his other crimes."

Charlie nodded at this but was not nearly so hopeful. This latest turn of events had shaken his confidence. He did intend to have a talk with Tito Alvarez and as soon as possible. It also occurred to him it wouldn't hurt to connect with Rupert Kly's sister Roberta, up in the

Chuskas. A long shot maybe, but something told him he should try. He wouldn't say anything about this to anyone, of course, not just yet anyway.

He and Fred stood a moment, watching as Irene and Billy Red Clay talked together. Harley and Thomas, leaning on the hood of Charlie's truck, glanced the couple's way from time to time, too, doing their best not to be too obvious.

All these men were probably wondering what sort of future the pair's relationship might hold for them. Not much of a future at all, in Thomas Begay's opinion. As he had stated before, he still thought it best his nephew and Irene go their separate ways. He couldn't imagine Billy Red Clay giving up his career in law enforcement to be a hanger-on to the Billy Moon entourage. Nor could he see Irene passing up the opportunity to be with her mother and sharing her luxurious and exciting lifestyle. No, he couldn't see any way either of these things could happen.

Charlie now had to admit, he didn't see it any other way himself. *No, in the end and regardless of outcome it would most likely be Billy Red Clay who wound up being the greater loser.* He also was aware what a great loss to his people it would be, should he decide to quit law enforcement, even if he had the opportunity. Charlie had watched him as he drew closer and closer to a real position of power in the Tribal police agency. In his own opinion, becoming liaison officer to the FBI had been the turning point in the young officer's career. There was nowhere else to go, but up.

14

Skullduggery

As so often is the case in the lives of ordinary people, extraordinary circumstances sometimes catch them unaware, occasionally changing their world in the most unimaginable way.

It was the morning after Charlie's last meeting with Billy Moon. He had no more than arrived at the office when Arlene buzzed him, saying Agent Smith was on the line and said it was urgent he speak with him.

"Yes, Fred, what's up?" The two had of late become very direct and to the point in their communications.

"Charlie, I've just come from the hospital. Tito Alvarez apparently went into cardiac arrest late last night and, despite the staff's best efforts finally passed away about thirty minutes ago. I arrived just as he was pronounced dead by the attending physician." The

Federal agent paused, and then went on without waiting for Charlie to respond. "The staff was under orders to call me immediately, night or day, should there be any change in his condition, and they did."

Charlie could hardly speak, "But, I thought his condition had stabilized. I called the head nurse every morning for a report...and each time was told 'he's showing steady improvement.' Only yesterday she said he had been moved out of ICU and into a private room downstairs. He shook his head. "This seems awfully sudden, Fred."

"I thought so too, Charlie, the Bureau's sending someone up from Albuquerque...should be here in four or five hours. He's our go-to medical expert and may be able to come up with something these local people missed. In any case, Tito's doctor will be out in a few minutes to give us his take on it."

"Have you notified Billy Moon?"

"Not yet, I haven't. I'll call her after I speak to the doctor in charge. I'm not looking forward to telling her, Charlie. She's not going to take it well, that's for sure."

The Investigator's mind was already ranging ahead to what effect this might have on the woman. "Damnit, Fred! I thought sure we'd have a chance to speak with the man. I was still hoping, when he got

266

better, he might remember something that would help. Silly of me I guess."

"I understand, Charlie, I was thinking along those lines myself…but, here we are." Fred paused, I'll keep you posted, of course, and let you know what the doctor has to say.

Charlie took a deep breath and then slowly let it out. "Thanks, Fred, I'll probably come in later to see what I might be able to do for Billy. It's going to be tough for sure. Thankfully, she's got Irene there with her. That should help."

After hanging up, the investigator found himself unable to get past this unexpected development. It just seemed illogical from any angle. He couldn't stop thinking about it. In less than ten minutes Fred called back.

"Charlie, I just talked to the doctor, and he's as puzzled as we are—he sees no apparent reason for this sort of complication and, in fact, says he had scheduled Alvarez for release in another day or two. He had already talked to Billy Moon about releasing him, and she assured him she would see to the man's care and recuperation. She apparently seemed quite happy with how well he was doing."

"Okay, Fred, I'm going to clear up a few things here and then head into town to see Billy. After how our last conversation ended, I'm not looking forward to it, but I owe the woman that much. I am, after all, still her advocate here at Legal Services. I don't know…I guess I'm feeling guilty for thinking we had such a lock on this case…and then, it all falls apart. It was a rookie thing to do, that's all."

"I wouldn't beat myself up over it, Charlie, we all thought we had this one in the bag. The Bureau won't give up. We still have the arson charges, those will stick. And on the other, there's still the old-fashioned way."

"You mean building a case based on circumstantial evidence?"

"It wouldn't be the first time, Charlie."

The investigator secretly shook his head, glad the agent couldn't see it. They both knew what a long shot that would be. After they hung up, Charlie grabbed his jacket, stopping only long enough to let Arlene know where he was going, asked that she field his calls for a couple of hours.

"Sure boss," she said, smiling, "I might wind up with your job one of these days anyway. If you're not careful."

Charlie laughed despite himself. "Arlene, I wish you did have this job…and I think you'd be good at it, too."

The woman stared after him and while she smiled at the idea, couldn't help entertaining the possibilities.

On his way into town, Charlie, revisited the thought of speaking to Rupert Kly's sister Roberta, wondering now just how much the woman knew of her brother's criminal past. She'd been Rupert's staunch supporter since they were children, until recently when, the entire clan turned against him. But had she really turned away from her brother now, or was it all just a smokescreen? *I wonder how well Billy Moon knew Roberta, or for that matter, what sort of relationship did Irene have with her aunt?*

Turning into the RV park, Charlie noted Billy Red Clay's police unit was not in its usual surveillance location. The investigator was still wondering about this as he rounded the corner and made his way up the narrow thoroughfare where Billy Moon's tour bus sat parked. He spotted the Tribal policeman's vehicle…parked just behind Fred Smith's government car. There was no sign of the rock star's tan colored Jeep. Fred and the Policeman stood talking at the front of the tour bus and only turned his way as he pulled to the side of the street. The two each raised a hand to him as he stepped out and made his way up the walk. Charlie had the immediate sense something was very wrong. Both men wore a serious expression and stopped speaking as he approached.

"Charlie, did you happen stop by the hospital on your way into town?"

"No, I didn't, what's up? Isn't Billy here?"

"No, she isn't, have you talked to her this morning?"

"I have not, Fred, I was just on my way up here to see her and try making some sort of amends."

"We don't know where she or her daughter are. Officer Red Clay here called me saying the mother and daughter sped by his surveillance post without even looking his way. I told him to stand by here until I arrived. Something's going on with those two, and it looks like they don't want us to know what they're up to." The agent pointed at the motor home. "The bus is locked up, and they unplugged the utilities before they left. You'll notice the jacks are not down either. It's as though it's been readied for a speedy departure." Fred smiled. "I checked with the park office, they're paid up in full, but didn't say when they would be leaving...or even if they'd be leaving. The manager said Irene had come in yesterday inquiring about taking the space on a long-term basis. Any idea what's going on with them?"

Charlie thought for a moment before admitting, "Fred I don't have a clue, but they obviously intend to come back for the bus.'

"Yes, you'd think so, wouldn't you? But Billy Moon's a very wealthy woman, Charlie, I suppose almost anything is possible in her situation."

So far Billy Red Clay had not said a word, but he cleared his throat, and stepped forward. "I don't think Irene would leave here for any length of time without letting me know where she's going."

Both older lawmen gave him a thoughtful gaze. Charlie said gently, "Billy, there's a good possibility she already has."

Realizing he may have sounded foolish, the young cop looked down for a moment, and in a more subdued tone said, "I suppose you could be right, Charlie."

Fred didn't look at the liaison officer, turning instead to the investigator. "Would you happen to know if Billy Moon kept any firearms?"

Charlie was caught a little off guard. "Uh…I don't think that ever came up in conversation, Fred, though I would imagine Tito Alvarez might have had one or two tucked away somewhere, given the nature of his work."

The agent nodded, "Tito owned two handguns and a sawed off 12 gauge, actually. That's according to what we could pull up from ATF files. All legally acquired and registered in his name. I would assume he kept them in the motor home."

271

Charlie grew thoughtful, "Well, he didn't seem to have a weapon in his possession when he was up at Glynda Benally's place. Nothing on him when we found him unconscious, either. You don't think these women are armed and dangerous, do you Fred? He said this in a joking manner but then quickly regretted it.

The agent wasn't smiling when he answered. "Just saying, Charlie. We don't know what these two have in mind…or how they intend to go about it."

"What the hell, Fred, they may have just been going out for breakfast or anything else, for that matter."

Fred considered this for a moment. "Do you believe that's what they are doing, Charlie?

The investigator paused then sighed, "No. I don't"

"I thought not… I understand not wanting to think the worst, but we do have to consider every possibility."

"I guess I just don't want to believe Billy Moon is irrational enough to go after Rupert Kly by herself…and certainly not make her daughter an accomplice." The investigator let out a deep breath. "On top of her other grievances, I'm sure Tito's death hit her pretty hard. Then there's the autopsy reports indicating the lack of iron-clad evidence against Rupert. That alone could have pushed her over the edge." Giving the FBI Agent a significant glance, Charlie went to his truck and picking up the two-way mic, had Arlene patch him through to Harley Ponyboy's place. Celia picked up and asked the investigator to hold while she called her husband to the phone. In only a few moments the man answered, "Hello, it's me."

Rolling his eyes, the investigator cut to the chase. "Harley, I have reason to believe Billy Moon and her daughter may be headed past your place shortly in their Jeep. Would it be possible for you to go down to your mailbox and keep an eye out for them. You may have to hang out down there for a bit. Don't try to flag them down or anything. In fact, if they do come by, pretend you didn't see them at all. Just call Arlene back and have her put you in touch with me. Can you do that for me, Harley? Oh, and we may need your services later if you're up for that?"

Charlie already knew what his answer would be. There was nothing Harley liked better than being involved in any kind of track and pursuit project of Charlies.

"I can do that for you, big guy." After a moment of silence he said, "You do remember Thomas and I telling you there was something not right about the woman, don't you?"

Charlie shook his head. "I remember, Harley…but I wouldn't get my hopes up…we don't know anything of the sort yet."

Fred and Billy Red Clay had heard some of the conversation, but Charlie filled them in, just to be sure everyone was on the same page. "If they go past, Harley, there's a good chance they're headed for the Chuskas. Irene may know something or someone up there who knows where Rupert's hiding out, or she may have figured it out herself. She knows a lot about the man that we don't."

Fred nodded. "I'll get a bulletin out on the vehicle, and you can alert Tribal police to be on the lookout too, Billy."

The policeman hesitated, and then offered this thought, "There is the possibility they might have been frightened by Tito's death and decided to leave the area until Kly is apprehended."

Charlie agreed this was a possibility and wondered why he hadn't already considered this himself, but still had a hard time putting fear and Billy Moon together in any context.

Fred conceded the point when he said, "I'm going back to my office, where I can coordinate things a bit better on my end. Billy, I'd appreciate it, if you would hang out here for a little longer, just in case the two should return for some reason." He smiled grimly, "Women are known to change their mind, you know."

Billy Red Clay could only hope the agent's comment wasn't a hint directed at him and Irene.

As Fred got in his car and left the RV park, Charlie and Billy moved closer to the investigator's radio to wait for Harley's call. The two men had stood and discussed the situation for no more than a minute or two before the truck's horn alarm went off, alerting them to an incoming call.

"Yes, Harley… No, you're coming in just fine… What's up? I see…that's good… I will head your way right now, be ready to go if you're still interested in coming along. No, I can't say when we might make it back." The investigator listened for another moment or so, then smiling, hung up the mic. Standing a moment in thought, he then turned to Billy Red Clay. "Well, those two just went by him, not more than ten minutes ago. They are heading for the Chuskas all right," he said, ignoring the fact that the women could just as well continue east on US 64, heading God knows where. "I've got a gut feeling about this, Billy. I knew these women couldn't be afraid of Rupert Kly. She intends to find the man herself, and when she does…she'll end it her way. It's what she's wanted from the beginning. If they should stop to ask questions of Irene's relatives, we may be able to catch up to them before they get into any real trouble. Billy, you can drop your car off at Legal or you can take it with you if you think we need to make a bigger splash when we get there."

Billy had never seen Charlie so excited; it was a little worrisome, but it was contagious. The policeman hurried off to his own vehicle, pausing to turn after only a few steps. "Do you think we should radio Fred and let him know where we're going?"

Charlie had just opened the door to his own car and stared silently at the radio a moment before turning his head to answer, he knew it was the liaison officer in Billy doing the talking. "Not just yet. Let's wait until we see what's going on up there. Once we're sure what's happening, we'll let him know."

Harley Ponyboy was waiting by his mailbox, with a large sack of sandwiches and two thermoses of hot coffee. He was ready for anything. "Thomas is going to be mad you didn't let him in on this."

"No time to wait for him. We'll be lucky to catch those two as it is."

As he glanced up the road, Harley spied the police vehicle coming up fast, and ran to the back of the truck just as Billy Red Clay skidded up behind. Reaching into his sack he grabbed a couple of sandwiches and one of the thermoses—which he pushed through the window to Billy. The policeman barely had time to thank him, before he was gone. Charlie's tires scattered gravel as he came back up onto the highway, making Billy frown at the clatter of little rocks on the front-end of his new unit. Both lawmen had their sirens blaring as they passed through Shiprock, letting people know they were coming and were serious about them clearing the way. The curious turned to watch as the two vehicles roared through town, probably wondering what disaster had befallen some poor soul.

Once outside town and on the Chuska turn-off, there was virtually no traffic. Charlie floored the Chevy while glancing back at Billy. The policeman's eyes widened as they hit numbers well over the speed limit. Approaching the trading post, they were surprised to see an on-coming pickup careen into the parking lot and stop in a cloud of dust at the trader's door. Harley Ponyboy glanced over at the investigator who nodded, "I think we better see what's happening!" Charlie flipped on the blue and red flashers as he hit the brakes. Billy Red Clay must have anticipated the move, as both vehicles came to a stop side by side near the building's entrance. The trader himself was already on his way out of the store wiping his hands on his apron as he watched a middle-aged woman get down from the truck, obviously in a wild-eyed state of anxiety. Everyone converged on her at the same time, confusing her to the point of speechlessness. The trader, who seemed to know the woman, moved to take her arm, comforting her in Navajo.

Recovering somewhat, she exclaimed in a high voice, "I had just come to call the law, but now I see they must already know." Zeroing in on the uniformed cop she asked Billy, "Did someone call you about the shooting?"

Billy Red Clay looked first at Charlie, and then back at the distraught woman. Having had a good deal of experience with people in such a state, the policeman answered her in a calm and respectful manner. "May I have your name, please?"

The woman looked at him a moment before taking a deep breath and saying, "My name is Emma Shorthair. I was passing the turn off onto the mountain road when a young man flagged me down to say a woman had been shot up at their camp, and would I report it to the trader or call the police myself?"

"Did this man say his name? Or, even who it was that was shot?"

"No, he didn't, only that he had to get back up there to his family. He said he hadn't been sure his truck had enough gas to make it to the trading post and was glad I came along when I did."

The trader guided the woman to a bench in front of the store, calling to his wife to bring a glass of water.

Charlie turned to Billy, who had spent some time with those people up in the Kly family camp. "Did you see this woman when we were last up there?"

"No, I've never seen her before. She said she was from farther out, toward Chaco Wash. She was talking so fast you might have missed that."

Charlie glanced at Harley, who confirmed the woman had mentioned it when she first got out of her vehicle.

Billy was again questioning Emma in Navajo. She had calmed down considerably and was now, apparently, beginning to enjoy being the center of attention. "That camp has always made problems for people around here. I knew Rosemary Kly when we were young. I always liked her, too. But that husband of her's was not anything like Rosemary. My husband heard he was back up there...my husband and I...we have a little band of sheep we pasture just north of them and one of the herders told him Rupert was back. I didn't see him myself; you understand."

Charlie caught what she'd said about Rupert Kly and nudged Billy. "Let's go, we may already be too late. I'll call Fred Smith...tell him what's going on, and that we'll likely need a helicopter up this way. We had good radio coverage up there the last time we were there, so that's better than using the trader's phone and having it broadcast to everyone in the area."

After calling in, and once again on their way up to the sheep camp, the three *Dinés*' thoughts were with Billy Moon and her daughter. Charlie's head was awhirl with the fear they might have been injured or even killed. He thought he should have seen this coming. After the discouraging autopsy reports on Rupert's wives, and the added shock of Tito Alvarez dying before he could tell them who the shooter was, it had all been too much for the already troubled rock star. Charlie had reasoned the finding of her daughter, after all these years, would be enough to placate her until he and Fred could put some sort of circumstantial prosecution together against Rupert. Both lawmen were still treating the deaths as murders. There was, of course, the arson and felony endangerment case to fall back on. They had enough witnesses to put Kly away for a long time on that felony charge alone. Neither of the two lawmen thought "Lucky" Kly would walk away from that almost certain indictment. The investigator was sure Fred Smith would have those indictments forthcoming as soon as possible.

As troubling as all these things were, Charlie was still confident they would apprehend the fugitive in a timely manner and hoped they might somehow obtain a confession on at least one of the suspected murders. The Legal Services investigator prayed there had not been a further killing to add to the list.

The road was as rough as the lawmen remembered it, and a long crawl to the top. This time, not knowing what to expect, they decided to take both vehicles. Harley agreed. In his opinion they might even have to split up at some point.

Making their way up to the first bench, they paused at the camp of Lester and Gladys Nez. It took only a few moments to realize the couple were not home. Charlie, clearly disappointed, said, "I had assumed we might get a better idea of what went on up top from these folks—and maybe get some idea how best to approach their relatives. Those people up there are already leery of lawmen, though the three of us being *Diné* may work to our advantage...I hope so anyhow."

Harley narrowed his eyes in thought. "I would imagine Lester and Gladys are up there with the rest of the clan and will likely help us put the others at ease. That young couple likes Billy Red Clay from what I've heard."

"Yes, Billy got on with them well enough and, that should be in our favor. Still, these folks back in here are often slow to gain confidence when it comes to cooperating with the law."

Breaking out over the rise brought them in view of the main camp. A small group of people were gathered in front of a *hogan*—their expressions mixed. Fortunately, Gladys Nez was in the forefront and first to come forward to greet the vehicles. Charlie rolled down the window and frowned as he saw Lester Nez standing at the open door of the *hogan,* blood on his hands and looking his way. Turning back to the man's wife and baby, he asked, "What's going on Gladys? We were told someone had been shot up here this morning?"

Gladys moved closer to the pickup and spoke in a low voice, "We've had a lot of excitement here, Mr. Yazzie. Rupert Kly came earlier, pounding on my Aunt Roberta's door. Most of the men, and some of the women, were out moving the sheep around at the time. One of my younger cousins saw my Aunt Roberta open her door and let him in. After a while, she said, there was a lot of loud arguing, and a few minutes later they heard a shot. Then Rupert came out and got in Roberta's truck and took off. My cousin went to the door and called for Roberta several times but didn't get any reply."

"No one went in to check on the woman?"

"No, my cousin said no one wanted to go in there…too scared of what they'd find, I guess. You know, Mr. Yazzie, most of my relatives are afraid of dead people and don't want to take a chance of a *Chindi* getting attached on them."

Charlie glanced over at Harley Ponyboy, who only shrugged and stared out the window.

The young woman, seeing her husband coming out of her aunt's *hogan*, shifted the baby to her other hip while making a motion with her chin for her husband to come over and do the talking.

Reluctantly, Lester walked over and came up to the window and with a somber expression, said, "Hi Charlie. Gladys's cousin came down to our place saying they thought Roberta had been shot. She ask us if we could come up and check on the woman, you know, to see how she was and all. None of the other men were up there at the time…I guess I was their only choice. They knew I'm not so traditional and don't fear the dead like some. I took some EMT courses with the Fire department in that town where I grew up, so they figured I might be able to help Roberta…if she wasn't already dead."

Charlie sucked in a breath and held it a moment before finally asking, "And, is she dead, Lester?"

"Well, I thought she might be at first, it was awful dark in there. She was laying on the floor, and I couldn't hear her breathing, but when I said her name, she could tell it was me and not Rupert. She sort of groaned and tried to turn over a little. My eyes were getting used to the dark, and I was able to put a pillow under her head and ask her where she was shot. She said she thought it was in her side, and that it was bleeding a lot. I grabbed a towel and made a compress to tie on it to help stop the bleeding. Then I heard your trucks coming and told her help was on the way."

Charlie let out a deep breath. "There's a helicopter on the way, Lester. You did the right thing."

The young man looked relieved and lowered his voice as he glanced back at the others. "I'm sure glad to see you, Charlie. I didn't want to get blamed for it if she died." Then, almost in a whisper, said, "I've heard that has happened before with these people."

Charlie nodded without expression. "Everything is going to be alright now, Lester. We're not going to let this woman die. By the way, did you see anyone else come up past your place today—two women in a tan Jeep maybe?"

"No, Charlie, you people are the only ones to pass by our place as far as I know, but that doesn't mean someone else could have come by."

Billy Red Clay had got down from his truck and came up to help reassure the young couple. Being trained as an EMT himself and having considerable actual experience, Billy offered to have a look at Roberta himself. He and Lester were back in only a few minutes. The policeman nodded at Charlie, saying, "It's not too, bad, Charlie. She's lost some blood, but the rescue team should be able to stabilize her for the flight back to the hospital. I think she's going to be fine now." Billy was obviously in a hurry to rejoin the search for Irene and her mother and did not want to get left behind to monitor a rescue operation, as had happened the last time they were called up here to the Chuskas.

Charlie, on the other hand, felt it important he speak to Roberta himself before they left. Billy walked back to the *hogan* with him but stood outside the open door to wait.

Inside, the investigator saw that the woman was on her bed, propped up by pillows and seemed alert, though her face appeared drawn from the ordeal. She didn't seem particularly happy to see him. "Officer Yazzie, I told you last time you were up here my brother wouldn't be coming back. I guess I was wrong. He needed money and my truck, which he got, but not without shooting me to get them. He had waited until everyone was out with the sheep—if the men had been here, he wouldn't have tried it."

Charlie nodded. "Where do you think he was going, Roberta?"

285

"Before we argued, he said he just needed some food, which I gathered up for him. Thinking I was on his side like always, he told me he was headed up to our old home place for a few days…until things cooled off. He asked me to send word if anyone came looking for him. When I didn't say anything to this, he grew angry—demanded my truck and what little money I had. We got pretty loud, I guess. I was hoping someone would come to help me, but the few women left here in camp were afraid of him and hoping he would just leave." Her voice trailed away, obviously the pain was becoming more intense.

Charlie assured her a helicopter and medical team was on the way. "They'll give you something for the pain and have you at the hospital in no time. You are going to be all right." He hesitated briefly before saying, "I have to tell you, Roberta, your niece, Billy Moon, and her daughter may already be up here somewhere, looking for Rupert. We need to know where he's at."

The woman gritted her teeth as she attempted to sit up. "Billy Moon knows where to find him. He used to take her there when she was young—I doubt she has forgotten the place." The woman turned away and didn't look at him again but said in a muffled voice, "Ask Lester Nez, he knows where the place is."

Charlie hurried to the door as Billy Red Clay held it open, saying, "I heard her. I'm sure Lester will show us the way."

When asked, Lester willingly agreed. "It's not all that far from here, but there's hardly any road left to speak of. It will take some time to work our way back in there."

Charlie frowned at hearing this but could only sigh and say, "I'm not sure we have any time left."

15

Redemption

Billy Red Clay had the better truck and was also the one who knew Lester Nez best. The investigator suggested these two men lead off. He and Harley would fall in behind them—cautioning the pair to stop well back from the dwelling itself. He didn't want the sound of the trucks heard in the camp. They would go in on foot, leaving Lester with the vehicles. Charlie didn't want to be responsible for a civilian…especially not a new father. Harley, he said, was in the employ of Legal Services, as it were, and an experienced hand at this sort of thing.

Lester had been right about the road, summer rains washed out whole sections, making the going not only hard but dangerous as well. They had been wise to bring both vehicles. He pointed out a narrow, rutted track coming in from the right at a steep angle. "That's the old way in, only someone who has lived here would know about it. It's the only way they could have got around our place, coming in. It would take a Jeep to get in this way."

Billy nodded and made a mental note of the alternate route.

Harley Ponyboy hung his head out the window and said he recognized the tire tracks of the vehicle in front of the police unit. He could only see bits and pieces of the tread marks he suspected were Billy Moon's Jeep. It was rugged going, and he seemed surprised at how little time it had taken them. He knew Charlie had been thinking the terrain would slow them down more than it had. He judged the Jeep to be less than an hour behind Rupert.

When Harley mentioned this, the investigator glowered at the road, saying, "Still, at this rate they'll be on him before we can stop them." Cursing under his breath he exclaimed, "Rupert is sure to be watching the way in."

Harley turned from the open window and shook his head. "We can only hope Billy Moon takes the time to think this through and not just go busting in on him." Then he added, "At least the man won't have his rifle, according to what Billy saw after the fire. but he might have that stolen pistol Fred's informant said he bought."

"I would hope those women have some sort of weapon with them. I can't imagine her coming for someone like this, unarmed. I'm sure Tito would have made sure she had something and knew how to use it." Charlie had fallen a bit behind the Tribal unit, to allow Harley to sort out the tracks. Up ahead, Billy's cruiser could be seen slowing to a stop at the edge of the trail. Charlie stood on his own brakes and Harley's head hit the window frame with a resounding 'thunk'. The tracker rubbed his forehead as he scowled and said, "How about a little warning next time? You almost took my head off!"

Ignoring him, Charlie said, "It looks like Lester thinks they may be close enough to the camp."

"Well, this would be a good place for us to pull over, right there, between those two little junipers."

Charlie nodded, saying he doubted it would matter if they blocked the road, but at least they would be out of sight.

Billy Red Clay motioned them to come ahead on foot, as he backed his vehicle into the underbrush and got down from truck. Lester was already out and peering through the trees.

Without asking, Harley opened the glovebox and passed the investigator his .38. "It's loaded I hope?"

"Yep, checked it before we started out this morning. And you've got yours, right?"

"Yes, I do, but I hope we don't have to use them. I never shot anyone you know."

"Well, let's hope it doesn't come to that," the investigator said, putting his S&W in his jacket pocket. The two men left the vehicle and hurried up the trail. Billy and Lester were already moving toward the Jeep.

Charlie couldn't hear what they were saying to one another, though the two were now only a short distance away. Lester was standing to one side of the vehicle and turned to Harley as he came up.

"The old family cabin where Rupert was raised is just around the bend up there. Still far enough away I doubt anyone heard us come in."

Billy Red Clay was staring into the Jeep at Irene. Opening the door, he took a short-barreled pump shotgun from between the seats. Irene looked over at him nodding her head at the gun "My mother left it with me, just in case he got by her. She said, all I had to do is point it in the general direction and pull the trigger."

Billy raised his eyebrows, shaking his head and murmuring, "That ought to do it, alright."

Charlie trudged up to see Irene get out of the passenger side door, obviously happy to see Billy Red Clay.

"Irene, how long has she been gone?"

The young woman's voice wavered and fell to little more than a whisper as she answered. "About twenty minutes, I guess. I wanted to go with her, Charlie, but she wouldn't let me!" The girl's face was tear streaked and fearful as she looked up the road. "She told me she would take her time working her way up there and try for the back door. She must have figured he'd be watching the front."

Billy Red Clay put his arm around the girl, and she reached for his hand—just as the muffled sound of a shot reached them.

Charlie called for Harley to stay there with Lester and the girl so Rupert couldn't get past them.

For once Harley didn't argue. Billy Red Clay gently pushed Irene toward them as he passed the shotgun to Lester. Latching on to the girl's arm the man quickly pulled her to a safe place behind the vehicle. All three crouched out of sight as they watched Officer Red Clay take out his service weapon. With Charlie by his side, the pair made their way around the bend in the road, running for the cabin as they kept low in the brush.

~~~~~~

Billy Moon took her time in the cool Autumn air, making her way along a hidden path through the woods. *Winter is nearly here*, she thought.

How well she remembered days like this. What a wonderful time of year for a young girl to explore…if it hadn't been for Rupert Kly. The first time he'd brought her here, he said he needed help cleaning the old place up, fixing a few things that had to be done before the snows came. It would do her good to get out and get some fresh mountain air, he'd told her with a smirk on his face.

Staying concealed in the scrub oak along a trickle of spring water, Billy marveled at the splashes of red and orange already painting patches on the green fringes bordering the old cabin. She peered through the oak leaves as she studied the old dwelling. Then turning her head slightly, she listened thinking she'd heard some sound in the distance. She closed her eyes, concentrating. Finally nodding, she became satisfied it was only the soughing of the breeze in the treetops. The pistol that once had belonged to Tito Alvarez was in her coat pocket, the weight of it comforting, as she recalled Tito's voice, insisting she learn to use it…just in case some need should arise. Not likely, she'd thought. Tito would always be around to take care of such things and he didn't need a gun. She'd once asked him why he even bothered having one around. "Oh," he'd replied, "some-day… I might be getting old and could use a little help with things."

The last time she'd gone to see Tito, the night they moved him to the private room on the first floor, it was then she admitted to herself the man had indeed grown old. Old and afraid…the inoperable tumor was taking its toll. There was only one thing she could do for that. Her money couldn't buy him out of it this time. Tito Alvarez was, for the first time in his life, struggling with his own fading faith in himself. He had, at last, come face to face with his own mortality.

Sitting at his bedside, Billy Moon had gazed silently at the softly whirring machines, marveling at the mysterious exchange of information recorded on them. The story of a man's ongoing struggle to survive, should one understand the language. Quietly, Billy reached down and unplugged them. The man took a deep breath and then, just as his eyes fluttered shut, seemed to smile a last time.

After a short while, and with tears streaming down her face, Billy plugged the connectors back in, and then quietly left the room for the back exit. Nurses came, finally, to see what the matter was, and as Billy headed for her car in the back lot, she stopped at his window. Standing in the flower-filled border, she watched the frantic efforts of the staff as they scurried about. But too late, she decided. Smiling at the man lying on the bed she said her last goodbye.

A chill draught of air caused Billy to shake off the painful memory as she glanced toward the cabin and a darkening sky. After a quick look around, she pulled the slim .380 automatic from her pocket, examined it briefly, clicking off the safety.

The promised afternoon cloudbank had begun to slide in from the northwest. Edging cautiously up under the little overhang above the back door, she searched the weathered cracks in the wood then peeked through the largest of them. It took a moment for her vision to adjust to the small, dank interior…and then, there he was. Just as she had imagined him so many times in her night-mares. A large, evil-looking man, but not so frightening as she'd remembered. His back was to her as he watched intently at the edge of the little rag-curtained window a pistol lying on the table within his reach.

There was no lock on the cabin door as far as she could see, only the crude latch to be lifted. She contin ued to watch for a moment and saw the man suddenly gather himself, leaning forward as though he had spotted something in the distance.

It was the momentary diversion Billy had been waiting for. Taking a deep breath, she silently lifted the latch and flung open the door. Rupert straightened in surprise as he turned and grabbed for the nearby gun. Billy Moon pulled the trigger just as Rupert brought his weapon to bear. With only a grunt of surprise, he took her bullet high in the chest, his own gun clattering to the wooden floor as he clutched at the wound.

Giving a roar of rage and despite the mortal hit, the man unaccountably rushed toward Billy. Caught in the act of trying for a second shot, the woman froze for an instant. Long enough for her hulking attacker to grab at the pistol, trying desperately to wrest it from her grip. The woman tore at his face with her free hand, and the two grappled as the automatic discharged—both fell back at the blast and Rupert Kly sank before her eyes, likely dead as he hit the floor.

With a great sigh, Billy steadied herself at the table and sat heavily into the single chair—not for an instant did she take her eyes off the man. A grim smile was on her lips as Charlie Yazzie barreled through the front door, followed closely by Officer Red Clay, both with weapons at the ready, breathless and instantly struck speechless at the sight.

The policeman kicked the gun away from the man on the floor, then went to one knee and checked for a pulse, knowing he wouldn't find one. Looking up at the Legal Services investigator, he shook his head.

Charlie turned to Billy Moon and, looking directly into her eyes, asked softly, "Are you all right, Billy?"

The woman smiled up at him as though in a dream, "I am now, Charlie," she whispered, "for the first time in a long while… I'm all right.

Officer Red Clay, still bent over the dead man, looked up slightly—his eyes widening as he rose to his feet. "She's bleeding, Charlie!"

Following the officer's gaze, Charlie saw the growing pool of blood coming from under the table and quickly reached to support the woman as her head sank forward. Trying to speak, the woman uttered only a small sound deep in her throat and was silent.

The two lawmen exchanged shocked glances as Charlie quickly laid a finger alongside her neck, searching for even the hint of a pulse. Finally, glancing at his friend, Charlie shook his head sadly and looked away as his eyes filled. They could hear a truck pull up outside and knew the others had come as fast as they could. Charlie moved to the open door, holding up a hand for them not to enter. Irene's face fell as she quietly sobbed for the mother she had barely known.

Looking up, Charlie saw snowflakes beginning to fall from a leaden sky and murmured, "I'll not leave her here alone with that person… FBI's forensics be damned."

Billy Red Clay brought a blanket from behind the seat of his vehicle, and the two of them wrapped Billy Moon and gently carried her to the truck.

17

The Dilemma

The morning after Billy's death, Charlie was at his desk when he ran across a large manila envelope from the woman in the morning mail. Not surprisingly, the postmark revealed it had been mailed several days before, and at least a day before her death. The envelope contained a sealed packet marked, 'To be opened only in the case of my demise.' Making clear, he believed, what Billy had in mind from the beginning.

While Charlie thought he had dissuaded the woman from acting on her own, that had clearly turned out not to be the case. The autopsy reports on the deaths of Rosemary and Glynda Kly—followed by the inconclusive evidence in the investigation into her father's death, had undoubtedly convinced her to attempt the final act of justice on her own.

The packet contained a notice from Billy's Albuquerque attorney's office, acknowledging her wishes to ensure her daughter, Irene, became the sole beneficiary of her considerable estate. There was a further granting of executive powers-of-attorney to Charlie himself, in the matter of deciding a suitable place on the reservation for her burial. He felt it likely Billy viewed this eventuality as a final "coming home." She went on to say Irene might want to remain in the area where she'd grown up and had friends and family. Perhaps, she suggested, the girl could use a portion of her inheritance in the pursuit of advancing opportunities for young people on the reservation, which might give her some greater purpose going forward. This she said, should be mentioned but left to her daughter's discretion.

The investigator was still thinking about these things, when his new line indicator lit up the intercom, this time complete with sound effects. Surprised, he chose not to wait for Arlene to pick up but answered the call himself. "Investigator Yazzie, how can I help you?"

"Charlie, it's Fred, have you got a few minutes, I'm not far away and would like to drop by, if you're not too busy?"

"Sure, Fred, fact is , I have a few things here that you might be interested in yourself."

Hanging up the phone the investigator turned to gaze out his back window. Billy Moon's body wouldn't be released for a few days yet, and he had a lot to do if he was to comply with the woman's final requests. As he began putting everything back in the envelope, a small handwritten note fell to the desktop. Staring at it a moment, he couldn't help feeling the notion that this woman was presaging his every thought.

Dear Charlie,

Just a quick personal note of appreciation for all you've done for us...both me and daughter. There is a check in the envelope as a small token of my regard for your many efforts to help. As time goes by, I hope you might take it in your heart to look in on Irene now and then to offer whatever advice you might think helpful. She and Billy Red Clay seem to have hit it off for now and hopefully that relationship will grow stronger with time. He seems a fine young man.

In any case, I cherish knowing you and your family and friends, and wish them all my very best.

Billy Moon.

Charlie put the letter down and took a deep breath as he heard the intercom signal announcing Arlene was again on the line.

"Yes, Arlene…?

"Fred Smith is here to see you, sir. Should I send him on back?"

"Please do, Arlene, and hold my calls, if you will."

Fred Smith was at the office door almost as soon as the investigator clicked off the intercom. Looking up from clearing his desk, Charlie motioned to him. "Come on in Fred…have a seat."

The two men sat a moment, regarding one another, and each could see the other had something on his mind.

Fred was the first to speak, "Go ahead Charlie, what I've got might take a while."

The investigator shrugged and smiled, pushing the envelope his way. He waited as the FBI agent went through everything in that meticulous manner he had come to expect from the Bureau. Finally, Fred nodded and sniffed, as he pushed the papers back.

"I think there may be something Billy Moon left out." Then quickly held up a hand that he might continue. "You'll remember I told you we had a medical expert from our office in Albuquerque up here looking into the rather "questionable" death of Tito Alvarez?" The agent paused a moment for Charlie to answer.

"I remember that quite well, Fred… I'm assuming this person has reported back with something everyone else missed…or maybe just misunderstood?"

"Well, yes, and no. Agent Richards, was a forensics expert and former medical examiner himself. He pretty much agreed with what our own local doctors pinpointed as the probable cause of Alvarez's death. Which was a gradual asphyxiation due to lack of oxygen. The nurses on duty that night who, by the way, were in the middle of a shift change at the time, verified there had been an equipment alarm in the man's room. But by the time it was noticed, the person sent to investigate found Tito nearly dead. Yet, the support system seemed to be back in order when they came in. The monitors were checked and found to be working as expected. "Do you follow me so far, Charlie?"

"Yes, I think I understand the sequence of events leading up to his death. Which, unless I'm missing something, are much as we had already surmised, Fred." Charlie knew the agent had more to tell and let him take his time.

"Agent Richards," he said, "has a reputation for being very thorough, Charlie, and after he left for Albuquerque, called me at the office saying there was a bit of minutia he'd meant to make me aware of. He went on to say he had been tired from his drive over, and after he put together his report there in the hospital room, it was just breaking daylight. He had gone over to the window and opened it for a breath of fresh air, thinking it might help him wake up. In the flower bed below the window, he noticed several small boot prints. He had forgotten all about them until he was on his drive back but wanted me to know just for the record." Fred gave the investigator a significant look. Seeing he had Charlie's full attention, he went on. "I immediately drove back out to the hospital, but by the time I got there. the sprinkler system had been on for nearly an hour. I could see some impressions there below Alvarez's room alright but couldn't say for certain if they were boot prints or not." Fred sat there staring at Charlie as though imagining what was going through his head.

"I know what you're thinking, Fred, and I don't disagree. You are thinking back to the boot print we saw at Rosemary Kly's death scene." Charlie frowned, "But still, that's somewhat of a stretch, don't you think?"

"Not anymore, I don't." He smiled slightly. "It was dark when we were on our way back, and we stopped at what we *thought* was the place Rosemary died, and even then, only for a minute or two. Billy Red Clay, who stayed behind that night, went down to the scene the next day with forensics. He had the good sense to call their attention to the boot print which they made a cast of."

Charlie could sense the Agent was on to something but was not sure it was something he wanted to hear. "I don't quite get where this is going, Fred. We don't know who made the supposed prints at the hospital. Nor do we know for sure who made the print up in the Chuskas that night. Correct?"

"We didn't then, Charlie. The coroner's report came in this morning…I brought you a copy." Fred reached in his inside suit pocket and pulled out three folded sheets of paper, which he passed across the desk.

Charlie opened the report and began reading. Cause of death was indicated as a gunshot wound to the femoral artery of the right leg—causing a massive loss of blood and probably in only a few minutes time. The examiner noted the woman was wearing rather tall western style boots, the right one of which, had been filled with blood. Charlie drew in a quick breath and nodded to himself.

That's why they hadn't noticed her bleeding out any sooner than they had.

The rest of the report was pretty much as he would have guessed. Looking up at the FBI man, and sighing heavily, he asked "So, where does that leave us exactly, Fred?"

"That's why I came out this morning, Charlie. The medical examiner needs a signed confirmation of the woman's identity from someone close to her. I didn't think you would want to subject Irene to that sort of thing and suggested you acting as her attorney might suffice. I know the woman is an internationally known star and known to millions, but these are the rules. Someone has to do it, and in this case, I thought you were best qualified." The agent paused. "And one other thing, Charlie, I have the cast of the boot print found at the scene of Rosemary's death. We can once and for all, see if her boot fits the cast."

Charlie knew arguing the point with the Senior FBI agent was out of the question. Fred Smith was, first and foremost, a man who didn't bend rules. Not for anyone. The investigator reached down and pushed Arlene's button on the intercom. "Arlene, I'll be out of the office for the next several hours, can you cover for me till noon?"

"Will do boss, not a problem."

~~~~~~

It was a quiet ride to the coroner's office, neither man having much to say. Charlie glanced off towards the Chuskas. A lowering sky foretold more snow in the offing for the higher elevations. Most of the people in the Kly camps would have moved down to their wintering grounds by now, leaving nothing but a vast solitude in their wake.

The medical examiner, a sallow faced middle-aged man met them in the front office still wearing a grey rubber smock as he pulled off his gloves. Glancing at the plaster cast Fred was holding he frowned. "What can I help you gentleman with?"

Fred stepped forward. "I'm Agent Smith with the Federal Bureau of Investigation. I spoke with someone this morning regarding the Billy Moon investigation. And this is Investigator Charlie Yazzie of the Navajo Nation's Legal Services office, he will be making the official identification of the deceased."

The doctor straightened slightly. "Yes, I recall being told of the conversation. You wanted to examine the belongings of the deceased, if I remember rightly?" He moistened his lips with the tip of his tongue. "I'm afraid, gentlemen, that won't be possible. I checked with my assistant after you called this morning and was told a relative had already picked up the belongings."

Even Fred looked surprised. "Oh, and that would have been the woman's daughter, I presume?"

"I believe that's correct." The man went to the front desk and asked the person in charge for the log-book. After a short, whispered conversation he returned to say, "As I thought, it *was* the woman's daughter, about three hours ago. We've been quite busy this morning, and I had not been informed earlier or I would have let you know. As for the identification of the remains, the daughter took care of that as well, when she was here this morning. And now, gentlemen, I must excuse myself…I was in the middle of a procedure that is time sensitive, I really do have to get back." He nodded goodbye to the pair and left without another word.

Fred stood a moment in thought—disappointment plain in his expression. Sighing heavily, he turned for the door and said to Charlie, "I think we'd better have a word with Irene, and I mean right now!"

<center>~~~~~~~</center>

Charlie had remembered this being Irene's day off and thought she might be at her mother's place despite there not being an answer at the tour-bus number. "If she's not there… Billy Red Clay might know where she is." Fred picked up the mic and asked the radio operator to patch him through to Billy's office at Tribal Police.

"Officer Red Clay here, how can I help you, Fred?"

"Yes, Billy, Investigator Yazzie and I were wondering if you might know where Irene could be found this morning. We're not getting an answer at the tour bus. We just had a couple of quick questions for her, shouldn't take more than a few minutes."

There was a slight pause. "I spoke to her a few hours ago, Fred. She said there were a couple of things she had to take care of in town this morning but should be back at the bus before noon. I was going to meet her later for lunch."

Fred raised his eyebrows at the investigator as he paused for a moment. "Thanks, Billy, it's almost twelve now. We'll go on over and wait for her…. she could be there already I suppose." Signing off, the agent glanced at the Tribal Investigator, an odd look on his face. "I have a strange feeling about this, Charlie, and I'm not sure why."

Pulling into the RV park, it was soon apparent Irene's old car was there, but her mother's Jeep was not. Fred parked in front of the bus and began to drum his fingers on the wheel. Charlie cocked his head and glanced in the rearview mirror. "Here she comes now Fred, and in a hurry it seems."

Fred shot a quick look at his side-mirror and nodded, "Indeed she is."

The Jeep's tires chirped as the woman swerved in beside them. The men got out of the government car and stood waiting for her.

Irene was first to say hello, and beckoning them to follow, unlocked the door and went inside. Turning first to Charlie, she gave him what appeared to be an inquiring glance, and then smiled as she waved at the FBI agent. Pointing to the couch she immediately moved to the galley where she began making coffee. Calling over her shoulder she said, "I hope coffee's alright?"

Both men nodded, and Charlie said, "It looks like you've had a busy morning, Irene." Privately, he was amazed at how quickly she had assumed her mother's persona and how much more mature that made her seem. Neither man said anything further until the young woman came with the tray and began pouring them cups of the steaming brew. Settling herself across from the two, she took a sip of coffee and letting out a deep breath, asked, "What can I do for you gentleman this morning…or rather, afternoon, I guess I should say."

This was a totally different girl from the one Charlie had seen sobbing her heart out the previous day. Or the girl waiting tables only a week or so before. She was her mother's daughter, there was no doubt of that—totally in control and confident in her every move.

"Irene, we have just come from the coroner's office where we were told you picked up your mother's belongings early this morning." It wasn't really a question and was said in a casual and unassuming manner, something Charlie had always been good at.

She didn't hesitate. "Yes, that's right, I called ahead, and they were kind enough to have the package ready for me in the office. Is there something wrong with that?"

"Oh, no, not at all Irene." She hadn't mentioned identifying her mother's body. Though there was no reason she should have. Charlie was, in fact, glad he was off the hook for that and had been secretly pleased she had taken it upon herself. He again felt a small wave of relief flow through him at the thought.

Fred, not one to dally about when on official business, got right to the point. "Irene, I wonder if we might have a look at the contents of that package?"

"Well, you certainly could, Agent Smith, if I still had it."

"Whatever would you have done with it, Irene?" Fred was surprised for the second time that morning, and it showed—a rare thing from the generally taciturn agent.

Irene looked directly at the two men and said calmly, "I burned everything…to ashes. It took me most of the morning to do it."

Charlie looked at her a moment, and then asked, "Was there a specific reason for that, Irene? The coroner's office would have taken care of it for you."

"Yes, they said they would, but Roberta advised me it would be a cleansing thing to do it myself, for both me and my mother."

Charlie's mouth fell open, "Your Aunt Roberta? You've talked to her at the hospital?"

"I did, last night, we had a long conversation. I told her all that went on up at the cabin. She was very sorry to hear about my mother." Irene brightened noticeably. "She is doing quite well though…all things considered."

Fred Smith interceded, saying in a genial manner, "Well, Irene, we'd best be running along then. We do appreciate your time this morning." Glancing over at Charlie, as he rose from the couch, the agent now seemed anxious to go. "Billy Red Clay mentioned he's meeting you for lunch today. I expect he'll be along any time now."

Charlie too rose, to say, "Irene, I have some paperwork for you to sign at some point, you should have it in a day or so. In the meantime, if there's anything I can help you with…you have my number."

Back in the car the two men sat a moment or two as each considered the latest turn of events. Fred spoke, finally, and in a pensive voice, said, "Well, Charlie, I suppose this about wraps things up, wouldn't you say?"

"I suppose so, Fred, I can't see anywhere else to go with it at this point. Not for Legal Services anyhow." Charlie knew Fred would keep it in the back of his mind like he always did when things weren't cut-and-dried. But, for him, he was ready to let it go. Oh, he thought he might have another little chat with Roberta Kly when she felt better, but not just now. His grandfather had often said one should let a sleeping dog lie, and he still felt it good advice. But then, this wasn't a sleeping dog, was it?

~~~~~~~

In the days following Billy Moon's burial in the small cemetery at the Episcopal mission, the chosen few in attendance were still under a malaise of shock and sadness. Irene, he thought, held up well. At the end of the service, she came forward and placed a single red rose on her mother's casket. Then watched with dry eyes as the remains were slowly lowered into the grave. For his part, Charlie still struggled with the guilt of being only minutes too late to save the woman's life

The sun shone down, from a brilliantly blue sky. It was a perfectly crisp, fall day. The investigator thought back to the day Billy Moon, raised her arms to a shower of falling leaves in a golden moment. He had done all in his power to prevent the tragedy. Still, his conscience was not appeased. Charlie knew thoughts of Billy Moon would linger on for a very long time.

Addendum

These stories hearken back to a slightly more traditional time on the reservation, and while the places and culture are real, the characters and their names are fictitious. Any resemblance to actual persons living or dead is purely coincidental.

~~~~~~

Though this book is a work of fiction, a concerted effort was made to maintain the accuracy of the culture and life on the reservation. There are many scholarly tomes written by anthropologists, ethnologists, and learned laymen regarding Navajo culture. On the subject of language and spelling, they often do not agree. When no consensus was apparent, we have relied upon "local knowledge."

Many changes have come to the *Dinè*—some of them good—others, not so much. These are the Navajo I remember. I think you may like them.

ABOUT THE AUTHOR

R. Allen Chappell is currently the author of thirteen novels and a collection of short stories. Growing up in New Mexico he spent a good portion of his life at the edge of the *Diné Bikeyah*, went to school with the Navajo, and later worked alongside them. He and his wife now live in Western Colorado where he continues to pursue a lifelong interest in the prehistory of the Four Corners region and its people, and still spends a good bit of his time in that area.

For the curious, the author's random thoughts on each book of the series are listed below in the order of their release.

Navajo Autumn

It was not my original intent to write a series, but this first book was so well received, and with many readers asking for another, I felt compelled to write a sequel—after that there was no turning back. And while I have to admit this first story was fun to write, I'm sure I made every mistake a writer can possibly make in a first novel. I did, however, have the advantage of a dedicated little group of detractors, quick to point out its deficiencies...

and I thank them. Without their help, this first book would doubtless have languished, and eventually fallen into the morass.

Navajo Autumn was the very first in the genre to include a glossary of Navajo words and terms. Readers liked this feature so well I've made certain each subsequent book had one. This book has, over the years, been through many editions and updates. No book is perfect, and this one keeps me grounded.

Boy Made of Dawn

A sequel I very much enjoyed writing and one that drew many new fans to the series. So many, in fact, I quit my day job to pursue writing these stories full-time—not a course I would ordinarily recommend to an author new to the process. In this instance, however, it proved to be the right move. As I learn, I endeavor to make each new book a little better…and to keep their prices low enough that people like me can afford to read them. That's important.

Ancient Blood

The third book in the series and the initial flight into the realm of the southwestern archaeology I grew up with.

This book introduces Harley Ponyboy: a character that quickly carved out a major niche for himself in the stories that followed. Harley remains the favorite of reservation readers to this day. Also debuting in this novel was Professor George Armstrong Custer, noted archaeologist and Charlie Yazzie's professor at UNM. George, too, has a pivotal role in many of the later books.

Mojado

This book was a departure in subject matter, cover art, and the move to thriller status. A fictional story built around a local tale heard in Mexico years ago. In the first three months following its release, this book sold more copies, and faster, than any of my previous books. It's still a favorite of readers here at home, and abroad.

Magpie Speaks

A mystery/thriller that goes back to the beginning of the series and exposes the past of several major characters, some of whom play key roles in later books and a favorites of Navajo friends who follow these stories. Di tradition is a theme that runs throughout this novel.

Wolves of Winter

As our readership attained a solid position in the genre, I determined to tell the story I had, for many years, envisioned. I am pleased with this book's success on several levels, and in very different genres. I hope one day to revisit this story in one form or another.

The Bible Seller

Yet another cultural departure for the series; Harley Ponyboy again wrests away the starring role. A story of attraction and deceit against a backdrop of wanton murder and reservation intrigue—it has fulfilled its promise to become a Canyon land's favorite.

Day of the Dead

Book eight in the series, and promised follow-up to #1 bestseller, "Mojado". Luca Tarango's wife returns to take his remains back to Mexico and inveigles Legal Services Investigator Charlie Yazzie to see that she and Luca's ashes get there for the Mexican holy Day of the Dead.

The Collector

Book number Nine in the series brings most of the original characters into play, but centers around Lucy Tallwoman. The murder of her agent causes her life to spiral out of control as unseen forces seek to take over the lucrative Native Arts trade. A fast-paced story that garnered many new fans for the series.

Falling Girl

Book ten—Reservation favorite Harley Ponyboy steals this one with his rags to riches tale of lost love, deception, and newfound happiness. A reservation adventure to warm the coldest heart.

Yellow Dirt

The eleventh book in the series takes the author back to his early days in the Four Corners country, and his first knowledge of the uranium industry on the reservation. While the book is heavily fictionalized, it remains true to the mood and story of those times. While many claims have been satisfied over the years, reparations to some individuals still are being pursued even today. As Cicero once noted: "The more laws, the less justice."

Dead Fall

The long-awaited sequel to the best-selling novel "Wolves of Winter." We invite readers to ride along in the timeless world of the Diné where the "Four Corners" marks the often-secretive realm of the Dinetah. Travel through soaring canyon walls to meet the ancients whose spirits linger still in the shadows of cliffside dwellings. Thomas Begay's son Caleb becomes obsessed with the ancient and mystical life of the Anasazi, even as he mourns a great personal loss in their family.

From the Author

We would remind our readers, we remain available to answer questions, and welcome your comments at: rachappell@yahoo.com

If you've enjoyed this latest story, please consider going to its Amazon book page to leave a short review. It takes only a moment and would be most appreciated.

Glossary

1. Adáánii — undesirable, alcoholic etc.
2. Acheii — Grandfather *
3. Ashki Ana'dlohi — Laughing boy
4. A-hah-la'nih — affectionate greeting*
5. Billigaana — white people
6. Ch'ihónit't — a spirit path flaw in art.
7. Chindi — (or chinde) Spirit of the dead *
8. Diné — Navajo people
9. Diné Bikeyah — Navajo country
10. Diyin dine'é —Holy people
11. Hataalii — Shaman (Singer)*
12. Hastiin — (Hosteen) Man or Mr. *
13. Hogan — (Hoogahn) dwelling or house
14. Hozo — To walk in beauty *
15. Ma'ii — Coyote
16. Shimásáni — Grandmother
17. Shizhé'é — Father *
18. Tsé Bii' Ndzisgaii — Monument Valley
19. Yaa' eh t'eeh — Common Greeting-Hello
20. Yeenaaldiooshii — Skinwalker, witch*
21. Yóó'a'háaskahh —One who is lost

*See Notes on following pages

1. Acheii — Grandfather. There are several words for Grandfather depending on how formal the intent and the gender of the speaker.

2. Aa'a'ii — Long known as a trickster or "thief of little things." It is thought Magpie can speak and sometimes brings messages from the beyond.

4. A-hah-la'nih — A greeting: affectionate version of Yaa' eh t'eeh, generally only used among family and close friends.

7. Chindi — When a person dies inside a hogan, it is said that his chindi or spirit could remain there forever, causing the hogan to be abandoned. Chindi are not considered benevolent entities. For the traditional Navajo, just speaking a dead person's name may call up his chindi and cause harm to the speaker or others.

11. Hataalii — Generally known as a "Singer" among the Diné, they are considered "Holy Men" and have apprenticed to older practitioners sometimes for many years—to learn the ceremonies. They make the sand paintings that are an integral part of the healing and

know the many songs that must be sung in the correct order.

12. Hastiin — The literal translation is "man" but is often considered the word for "Mr." as well. "Hosteen" is the usual version Anglos use.

14. Hozo — For the Navajo, "hozo" (sometimes hozoji) is a general state of well-being, both physical and spiritual, that indicates a certain "state of grace," which is referred to as "walking in beauty." Illness or depression is the usual cause of "loss of hozo," which may put one out of sync with the people as a whole. There are ceremonies to restore hozo and return the ailing person to a oneness with the people.

15. Ma'ii — The Coyote is yet another reference to one of several Navajo tricksters. The word is sometimes used in a derogatory sense or as a curse word.

18. Shizhé'é — (or Shih-chai) There are several words for "Father," depending on the degree of formality intended and sometimes even the gender of the speaker.

20. Yeenaaldiooshii — These witches, as they are often referred to, are the chief source of evil or fear in

traditional Navajo superstitions. They are thought to be capable of many unnatural acts, such as flying or turning themselves into werewolves and other ethereal creatures; hence the term Skinwalkers, referring to their ability to change forms or skins.

Filename: Billy Moon .docx

Directory: /Users/Navajo/Library/Containers/com.microsoft.Word/Data/Documents

Template: /Users/Navajo/Library/Group Containers/UBF8T346G9.Office/User Content.localized/Templates.localized/Normal.dotm

Title:

Subject:

Author: Ron Chappell

Keywords:

Comments:

Creation Date: 10/17/23 11:31:00 AM

Change Number: 2

Last Saved On: 10/17/23 11:31:00 AM

Last Saved By: Ron Chappell

Total Editing Time: 1 Minute

Last Printed On: 10/17/23 11:31:00 AM

As of Last Complete Printing
    Number of Pages: 343
    Number of Words: 69,741
    Number of Characters: 311,194 (approx.)

Made in the USA
Las Vegas, NV
23 October 2023

79552780R10193